A STAR IS BORN
1937

A STAR IS BORN
1937

Published 2024 by Maple Spring Publishing

Front cover design by David Rheinhardt of Pyrographx
Interior design by Jason Snyder

Library of Congress Cataloging-in-Publication Data is available upon request

ISBN: 979-8-3505-0113-1

10 9 8 7 6 5 4 3 2 1

A STAR IS BORN
1937

Screenplay by Dorothy Parker, Robert Carson,
and Alan Campbell
Story by William A. Wellman *and* Robert Carson

CAST

Janet Gaynor *as* Esther Blodgett/Vicki Lester
Fredric March *as* Norman Maine
Adolphe Menjou *as* Oliver Niles
May Robson *as* Grandmother Lettie Blodgett
Andy Devine *as* Daniel "Danny" McGuire
Lionel Stander *as* Matt Libby
Owen Moore *as* Casey Burke
Peggy Wood *as* Miss Phillips
Elizabeth Jenns *as* Anita Regis
Edgar Kennedy *as* Pop Randall
J. C. Nugent *as* Mr. Blodgett
Guinn "Big Boy" Williams *as* Posture Coach
Clara Blandick *as* Aunt Mattie (*uncredited*)
Jonathan Hale *as* Judge George J. Parris (*uncredited*)
Marshall Neilan *as* Bert (*uncredited*)

$$\sim \!\! \mathcal{O} \mathcal{C} \!\! \sim$$

In the moonlight, we see a long expanse of snow. In the background, the isolated house of the Blodgetts in North Dakota. We hear the melancholy howling of the wolf.

Inside the Blodgett house, Aunt Mattie opens the door for Esther and Alec.

AUNT MATTIE

Well, home from the movies at last.

ESTHER BLODGETT

Looks like it, Aunt Maddie.

AUNT MATTIE

Huh?

ALEC

Hello, Dad.

MR. BLODGETT
(voiceover)

Hello, son. Well, daughter, how was the moving picture tonight?

ESTHER BLODGETT

Mm, lovely.

Esther, Alec, and Aunt Mattie go into the living room, where Mr. Blodgett is sitting.

ALEC

Mush. That's what it was. Just a lot of mush. There wasn't anybody killed in the whole thing.

Mr. Blodgett is looking through one of those old photo viewers.

MR. BLODGETT

Oh, well, then I'll stick to these; these don't talk.

ALEC

And that big cluck, Norman Maine, was in the picture tonight. Never does anything but kiss a lot of girls.

ESTHER BLODGETT

Norman Maine is one of the best actors in pictures.

AUNT MATTIE

You and your movies. That's all you think about. You shouldn't be allowed to go to them at all, if you're asking me.

Grandmother Lettie Blodgett comes in from the dining room.

GRANDMOTHER LETTIE BLODGETT

Too bad, I was so busy in the kitchen, I didn't hear anybody asking you.

ESTHER BLODGETT

Well, hello, Granny.

GRANDMOTHER LETTIE BLODGETT

Hello, darling.

AUNT MATTIE

But of course, no one ever listens to me.

GRANDMOTHER LETTIE BLODGETT

They do if they're within 10 miles of you.

AUNT MATTIE

Gathering around picture shows. Household cluttered up with movie magazines. And the other day I caught her talking to a horse with a Swedish accent!

MR. BLODGETT

Well, sis, we're only young once, you know.

Aunt Mattie sees Esther paging through a movie magazine.

AUNT MATTIE

Ah, Hollywood! You'd better be getting yourself a good husband and stop moaning about Hollywood. Do you know what she wants to do? She wants to go to Hollywood. I've known it all along. I've seen her making faces in the mirror and talking to herself. That's what comes of your movies.

MR. BLODGETT

Why? What would you do if you did go to Hollywood?

ESTHER BLODGETT

I'd be an actress. I would, I tell you, I've always known I could.

ALEC

Guys, wouldn't it be wonderful to have a movie star in a family? Oh, Miss Blodgett, may I have your autograph?

GRANDMOTHER LETTIE BLODGETT

You may not know it, Alec, but you're practically on your way to bed.

ALEC

Oh, Miss Blodgett, you're my favorite actress; won't you tell me the secret of your success?

ESTHER BLODGETT

Oh, let me alone.

Grandmother Lettie takes Alec off to bed.

MR. BLODGETT

Why, Esther, what's come over you?

AUNT MATTIE

I'll tell you what's come over her. She's just a silly little girl whose head has been turned by the movies. And the soon as she forgets the whole thing, the better off she'll be.

ESTHER BLODGETT

Why will I be better off? What's wrong with wanting to get out and make something of myself? What do you do that's so much better? Just because you're satisfied to sit here all your life, you think you can laugh at me? Well, someday you won't laugh at me. I'm going out and have a real life. I'm going to be somebody.

Esther dashes upstairs.

MR. BLODGETT

You know, if it was spring, I'd say give her a good dose of sulfur and molasses.

Esther is crying in her bedroom. Grandmother Lettie comes in.

GRANDMOTHER LETTIE BLODGETT

I thought I'd find you up. Ah, stop that. Now, stop crying. That isn't going to do you a bit of good.

ESTHER BLODGETT

Oh, I'm crying because Aunt Mattie and Alec make me so mad.

GRANDMOTHER LETTIE BLODGETT

Well, Alec and Aunt Mattie, they're not important. You are the only one that counts. Esther, everyone in this world who has ever dreamed about better things has been laughed at; don't you know that?

ESTHER BLODGETT

I suppose I do, but . . .

GRANDMOTHER LETTIE BLODGETT

But there's a difference between dreaming and doing. The dreamers just sit around and moon about how wonderful it would be if only things were different. And the years roll on, and they grow old, and by and by, they forget everything, even about their dreams.

ESTHER BLODGETT

I don't want to be like that; I want to be somebody.

GRANDMOTHER LETTIE BLODGETT

Oh yeah, oh yeah. You want to be somebody, but you want it to be easy. Oh, you modern girls give me the pain. When I wanted something better, I came across those plains in a prairie schooner with your grandfather. Oh, everyone laughed at us as they did at all the other pioneers. They said this country would never be anything but a wilderness. We didn't believe that. We were going to make a new country. Besides, we wanted to see our dreams come true.

ESTHER BLODGETT

Oh, Granny, it must have been wonderful.

GRANDMOTHER LETTIE BLODGETT

It was wonderful. But don't you think for one single minute that it was easy, Esther Blodgett. We burned in summer and we froze in winter, but we kept right on going, and we didn't complain because we were doing what we wanted to do. Can you understand that?

ESTHER BLODGETT

Yes, I can.

GRANDMOTHER LETTIE BLODGETT

Could you do it? Could you do it even if it broke your heart? Because remember, Esther, for every dream of yours that your make come true, you'll pay the price in heartbreak. Oh, I know what I'm talking about. You may not believe it, but I was a young girl once, and a very pretty young girl. A lot prettier than you are. And I was in love with your grandfather. And when some Indian devil put a bullet through him, that was as if it come right straight through my heart too. But I remembered all he taught me, and I went right on. I buried him out there in that wilderness with my own hands. And I went right on that same day. And I kept right on, even when your mother was born.

ESTHER BLODGETT

Oh, Granny. I want to make it worthwhile.

GRANDMOTHER LETTIE BLODGETT

You know, Esther, they'll always be a wilderness to conquer. Maybe Hollywood's your wilderness now. From all I hear, it sounds like it, but if you've got one drop of my blood in your veins, you won't let Mattie or any of her kind break your heart. You'll go right out there and break it yourself. That's your right.

(They hug.)

Here, oh, here, stop that nonsense.

Grandmother Lettie hands Esther a roll of bills.

GRANDMOTHER LETTIE BLODGETT

Here, take this and go to your Hollywood.

ESTHER BLODGETT

Oh, I can't take your money.

GRANDMOTHER LETTIE BLODGETT

Well, why not?

ESTHER BLODGETT

It's your savings.

GRANDMOTHER LETTIE BLODGETT

Well, I was only saving up for my funeral. Now I don't think I'm ever going to die.

ESTHER BLODGETT

Oh, Granny, how can I ever thank you?

GRANDMOTHER LETTIE BLODGETT

By giving me your word of honor that you will never tell a living soul where you got that money.

ESTHER BLODGETT

I promise.

GRANDMOTHER LETTIE BLODGETT

Remember, if you do, I'll have you arrested for robbing me.

As Grandmother Lettie leaves the room, Esther beams in gratitude.

The scene changes to the train station. A train whistle blows. It is snowing. Esther and Grandmother Lettie arrive in a carriage and get out.

ESTHER BLODGETT

Here, we are. Can I help you, Granny?

GRANDMOTHER LETTIE BLODGETT

Oh, I can live with it. Oh, my, it's cold.

ESTHER BLODGETT

I kissed Dad goodbye, just a little kiss. He didn't even wake up.

GRANDMOTHER LETTIE BLODGETT

I bet you didn't try that on your Aunt Mattie.

ESTHER BLODGETT

Oh, Aunt Mattie. Think of her face when you tell her.

GRANDMOTHER LETTIE BLODGETT

I am thinking about it. I've waited for that chance for 30 years.

TRAIN ATTENDANT

Here she is, girls.

The train attendant takes Esther's bag and moves off toward
the train.

GRANDMOTHER LETTIE BLODGETT

Oh, thank you. Come on, come on. Here's your prairie
schooner.

Esther and Grandmother Lettie approach the train, which is
pulling into the station.

TRAIN ATTENDANT

All aboard!

Esther and Grandmother Lettie hug each other.

ESTHER

Oh, Granny!

GRANDMOTHER LETTIE BLODGETT

Go on, go on, go on.

Esther boards the train and waves to her grandmother.

ESTHER BLODGETT

Goodbye, Granny.

GRANDMOTHER LETTIE BLODGETT

Goodbye. I'll be waiting for you in those moving pictures. Don't tell Mattie. You know my eyes are not as
good as they used to be, but my ears are all right. So,
you remember, talk up good and loud!

TRAIN ATTENDANT

All aboard!

ESTHER BLODGETT

Goodbye.

GRANDMOTHER LETTIE BLODGETT

Goodbye.

They wave at each other. The carriage driver comes up to Grandmother Lettie.

CARRIAGE DRIVER

Do you want go home now?

GRANDMOTHER LETTIE BLODGETT

I don't want to, but I will.

On screen, we see a legend: *"Hollywood . . . the beckoning El Dorado. Metropolis of Make-Believe in the California Hills . . ."*

A montage of Hollywood scenes: A hotel poolside, filled with people. Two male swimmers dive off a diving board, a beautiful young woman lying at poolside. The camera moves back to show a filming crew. A bus with the destination "Los Angeles" pulling into a depot. The train called "The City of Los Angeles" pulling into a station. An airplane, also called "The City of Los Angeles," lands at an airport.

Grauman's Chinese Theater: Esther walks in front of the theater, looks up, and marvels. She looks at autographs and footprints scratched into the concrete sidewalk with the names, autographs, and footprints of stars: Jean Harlow, Harold Lloyd, Joe E. Brown, Shirley Temple, Eddie Cantor, and finally one that says, "Norman Maine. Good luck." She steps into his footprints in the concrete and feels a thrill.

Now we see a classified ad: *"Rooms for Rent. Hollywood. $6 WEEKLY—Large rooms, running water. No cowboys. Convenient to all studios. Oleander Arms, 1312 Marion St., nr. Hollywood Blvd."*

Esther, with her suitcase, strolls into the lobby of the Oleander Arms. Mr. Randall, is at the desk, writing and smoking a pipe. He does not notice her. She comes up to the desk and rings the buzzer, startling him.

ESTHER BLODGETT

Good afternoon.

MR. RANDALL

Day, week, or month?

ESTHER BLODGETT

Well, it's a little hard to say. You see, I'm going into the movies.

MR. RANDALL

Well, you better take it for a week. It'll break your jump to Beverly Hills.

ESTHER BLODGETT

Are all the studios really near here?

MR. RANDALL

All except Gaumont-British.

ESTHER BLODGETT

I suppose the best way to get a job is to go straight to the studios, isn't it?

MR. RANDALL

Mm-hmm.

ESTHER BLODGETT

I haven't any illusions, you know. I'm perfectly willing to begin with a little bit of a part, or even as an extra.

MR. RANDALL

$6, please, in advance.

ESTHER BLODGETT

Oh.

She pulls the money out of her purse. Mr. Randall, still smoking his pipe, tries to peer into the purse, but, being noticed, averts his gaze.

We now see a printed note: "Miss Esther Blodgett: Your application for extra work received. All extra talent is engaged by this studio, as well as by all other major studios, through the Central Casting Corporation at 5504 Hollywood Boulevard, Hollywood California. —Paramount Pictures Inc."

Then we see Esther standing in front of a sign that says, "Do you understand figures? Extras Registered with us: Women—5,393; Men—5,517, Children—1,506. Total 12,416. This is more than SIXTEEN TIMES as many as we can use each working day. —July 1935. Central Casting Corporation."

Now apprehensive, she stands out in front of the Central Casting door, straightening her dress. Then she goes into the office, closing the door behind her. She approaches the receptionist at the desk.

ESTHER BLODGETT

I beg your pardon. I'd like to register for extra work.

RECEPTIONIST

How long have you been in Hollywood?

ESTHER BLODGETT

Well, it's about a month now.

FEMALE SPEAKER

We haven't put anyone on our books for over two years.
Come here. I'd like to show you something.

The receptionist leads Esther into a booth filled with telephone operators at a switchboard.

SWITCHBOARD OPERATORS

Central casting. Try later. Central casting.

RECEPTIONIST

Every time you see one of those little lights flashing, it's somebody asking for a job. Every time you hear them say, "Try later," it means there isn't any job. You can't keep the girls at the switchboard long; they'd go crazy. Every one of those little lights thought it was going to be a star. You still want to go in the movies? You know what your chances are? One in a hundred thousand.

ESTHER BLODGETT

But maybe I'm that one.

Esther goes out the office door.

Now we see Esther at the lobby of the Oleander Arms. Mr. Randall is working at his desk. She approaches.

ESTHER BLODGETT

Any phone calls for me, Mr. Randall?

MR. RANDALL

No. Jesse Lasky and Sammy Goldman must be writing letters instead. How was the luck today?

ESTHER BLODGETT

There wasn't any.

MR. RANDALL

Maybe you don't go at it in the right way.

Danny McGuire comes down the staircase near the desk.

MR. RANDALL

Take Danny McGuire here. He knows the ropes, don't
you, Danny?

DANIEL "DANNY" MCGUIRE.

Sure. I've had them around my neck for years.

MR. RANDALL

Huh? What? Oh Ms. Blodgett, Danny McGuire, our
new tenant.

ESTHER BLODGETT

How do you do?

MR. RANDALL

Mr. McGuire is a big director.

**Danny McGuire looks puzzled, then gets the joke and smiles
provocatively at Esther.**

ESTHER BLODGETT

Oh, are you really? Oh, could you possibly use me
in a picture, Mr. McGuire? Of course, I haven't had
much experience, but I don't think that really matters,
if you're willing. And I really feel that . . .

DANIEL "DANNY MCGUIRE

Now, listen lady, in the first place, I'm not a director.
I'm an assistant director. In the second place, if I had
any jobs to give away, I'd confer one on myself. And in
the third place, you should have stayed back home in
the first place.

Danny and Mr. Randall give definitive nods to each other.
Esther rushes up the staircase in tears.

MR. RANDALL

Oh, now look at what you've done.

DANIEL "DANNY" MCGUIRE

Hey, wait a minute!

Danny rushes up the stairs. In the second-floor hallway, he
finds Esther unlocking her room. He stops her from going in.
She stands at the doorway, sobbing. He blots her tears with a
handkerchief.

DANIEL "DANNY" MCGUIRE

Hey, don't be that way. Don't do that. Gosh, I didn't
mean to get tough. But a guy thinks he's being kidded
when somebody asked him for a job and he hasn't got
one for himself. After all, I'm not a big enough shot to
hurt your feelings.

He takes out a handkerchief and wipes away her tears.

ESTHER BLODGETT

I'm sorry. It wasn't just that. It was a lot of things—
looking for a job every day and never getting any nearer
to it. I guess I was beginning to get a little scared.

DANIEL "DANNY MCGUIRE

I know. Lady, do I know! Well, there's only one thing to do with that feeling when you're tired and sunk and down to your last nickel. Come on, and I'll buy you a drink.

ESTHER BLODGETT

Well, it's not as bad as down to the last nickel. I've still got $11 left.

DANIEL "DANNY" MCGUIRE

$11! You are going to buy me a drink. Come on.

Close-up of a bartender pouring two shots of rum into a glass of milk.

DANIEL "DANNY" MCGUIRE

That's right, George. There's nothing like a little rum to take away the milk flavor.

Now we see Danny and Esther at the bar. They jostle each other amiably with their elbows. He almost knocks her off her stool.

DANIEL "DANNY" MCGUIRE

I beg your pardon!

ESTHER BLODGETT

Same here. And when I sign my contract, the first thing I'm going to do is see that you direct every picture I'm in.

DANIEL "DANNY" MCGUIRE

That's my pal.

ESTHER BLODGETT

Of course, I'm going to be perfectly nice about it, but I'll just insist.

DANIEL "DANNY MCGUIRE

Now, that's the way to talk. Don't let them lick you.

ESTHER BLODGETT

Oh, I should say. They can't lick me if they try anything like that. I'll just won't sign.

DANIEL "DANNY MCGUIRE

Now, that's right. What have you got to lose? Another one of these, and we'll open our own studio.

They raise and clink their glasses.

Now we see a bill from the Oleander Arms, addressed to "Miss Esther Blodgett, Room #2." A voiceover from Mr. Randall reads out the rest of it.

MR. RANDALL

Bill rendered $24, past due. Remit without further delay. The Management. Me.

He stuffs the bill into a pigeonhole behind him, rubs his head, mutters, and slams his fist down in frustration. He pulls the bill out, tears it up, and tosses it behind him. Then he goes back to his Racing Form, muttering.

MR. RANDALL

Fifth race, fifth race . . .

Now we see a large sign that says, "Hollywood Bowl."

Then we see the bowl itself. In the background, the orchestra is tuning up. We zero in on Danny McGuire and Esther in the audience, looking through the concert program.

DANIEL "DANNY MCGUIRE

Hey, the program's going to be swell tonight. Now you take this fellow Beethoven. I'm a pushover for him, and Chopin, well, he is not so dusty either. But I kind of wish that once in a while, they'd play something you could sort of go out whistling, you know, like *[he blares out some song]*. Well, there's a tune. Hey, why don't you throw your hat in the air or something, can't you? This is a celebration. My job starts tomorrow.

ESTHER BLODGETT

I know it does. And I think it's swell, Danny.

DANIEL "DANNY MCGUIRE

Gee, I wish you were in on it too, but, oh no. It would have to be a war picture. One of those big novelty numbers. A war picture without any beautiful women at the front. Oh well, something will happen soon.

ESTHER BLODGETT

Maybe.

DANIEL "DANNY MCGUIRE

Why don't you go home, kid?

ESTHER BLODGETT

Oh, Danny, I can't do that. I came here, and I've got to stay.

DANIEL "DANNY MCGUIRE

Well, now if it's on account of money, I can always . . .

ESTHER BLODGETT

Thanks, but you've given me enough already. Anyhow, this is no time to be worrying. This is a party. Look at all the people, everybody in the world. Look, that's Norman Maine.

They see Norman Maine enter in evening dress, with a glamorous woman, Anita Regis, also in evening dress. He stumbles and steadies himself on her, almost pulling her down with him.

DANIEL "DANNY MCGUIRE

And he seems to have had that one extra cocktail.

As Norman and Anita take their seats, the audience starts to applaud. Before sitting down, he raises his arms, his fists clenched together overhead, like a boxer who has just won.

NORMAN MAINE

Oh, thank you.

ANITA REGIS

Sit down, you dope. That's for the orchestra leader.

NORMAN MAINE

Oh, right.

Esther and Danny notice this episode and laugh. Norman Maine sits down unsteadily. Behind him is Otto, a photographer with a camera and a large flash.

OTTO

Oh, Mr. Maine, Mr. Maine. Put your arm around Miss Regis.

NORMAN MAINE

Otto, this is the Hollywood Bowl.

OTTO

Oh, afraid of crowds?

NORMAN MAINE

Go on, go on, get out of here.

OTTO

What's the matter? You're getting too big to bother with photographers?

NORMAN MAINE

I don't want any pictures taken now.

OTTO

Oh, is that so? What's a person? I'll take it anyway.

NORMAN MAINE

I'll shove that Brownie number two of yours down your throat.

OTTO

No thank you, Mr. Maine.

Norman Maine gets up, seizes the camera, and dashes it to the ground. The two men begin to fight. A melee ensues, and several policemen arrive to subdue Norman. He backs off, and the police go away. We see Esther and Danny. He finds the scene funny, but she is disturbed.

ANITA REGIS

Normy, come back and sit down; everybody's laughing at you.

Norman and Anita go back to their seats and sit down. Norman misses his seat and falls down. Anita helps him into it.

Is he always like that?

DANIEL "DANNY MCGUIRE
I suppose he has to sleep sometime.

ESTHER BLODGETT
Oh, and he's so wonderful on the screen.

Norman Maine, a few rows in front of them, hears them, turns around, and hushes them, indicating that the orchestra is about to begin. Esther is disturbed, but still pleased that he has paid her some attention. Norman Maine scowls at them and turns to listen to the orchestra.

Now we see a letter on the stationery of the Oleander Arms and Esther's handwriting: ". . . and thanks again, dear Granny, for the money—but you mustn't keep sending it. Everything is going beautifully now. In fact, Daniel McGuire, the director, says I'm certain to get a job very soon."

We see Esther at the desk in her room, finishing the letter. She hears a knock.

ESTHER BLODGETT
Come in.

Danny comes in, looking disheveled.

ESTHER BLODGETT
Hello, Danny. What's the matter?

DANIEL "DANNY MCGUIRE
Well, believe it or not, I got a job for you.

ESTHER BLODGETT
Danny, that's wonderful. When do I go to the studio?

DANIEL "DANNY MCGUIRE

Well, you don't exactly go to the studio.

ESTHER BLODGETT

Oh, it's on location?

DANIEL "DANNY MCGUIRE

Well, it's not exactly on location.

ESTHER BLODGETT

But of course I haven't any makeup. Will you tell me what to get and sort of help me put it on?

DANIEL "DANNY MCGUIRE

Well, you don't exactly need any makeup. You see, it's not really a picture job. It's . . . well, it's being a waitress.

ESTHER BLODGETT

Oh.

DANIEL "DANNY MCGUIRE

Well, it's kind of a picture job if you look at it right.

ESTHER BLODGETT

You said it was a waitress.

DANIEL "DANNY MCGUIRE

Well, it's waitressing for Casey Burke, the big director over at our studio. He is giving a party tonight to kind of celebrate on account of kind of finishing the picture. And he wanted me to get him an extra waitress. And it's $5. And I thought of you right away, Esther.

ESTHER BLODGETT

That was awfully sweet of you, Danny.

DANIEL "DANNY MCGUIRE

Well, there are going to be a lot of big people at Burke's house tonight, and I'll bet you there's any number of big directors. And if you're there, maybe they'll notice you.

ESTHER BLODGETT

I could make them notice me.

DANIEL "DANNY MCGUIRE

Sure, you could. Esther; it's your chance.

ESTHER BLODGETT

My chance. All right, Danny, I'll do it. Oh, oh. But I can't, I haven't got the right things to wear.

Danny pulls out a waitress costume from a bag.

DANIEL "DANNY MCGUIRE

Now you don't think the wardrobe department's right next to my office for nothing. Do you?

She holds up the dress in front of her.

DANIEL "DANNY MCGUIRE

A perfect fit.

In Casey Burke's living room, we see a very stuffy-looking butler with muttonchops and in evening dress coming into the living room, bearing a tray of drinks and hors d'oeuvre. Esther, in maid's costume, follows, bearing a small tray with hors d'oeuvre. Two men in evening dress are standing and chatting.

MALE SPEAKER

Did you get to the preview last night?

MALE SPEAKER #2

I did.

Esther comes toward them, bearing her tray and mincing in the most ridiculous fashion.

ESTHER BLODGETT

(in some semblance of a European accent)

Would you like a leetle hors d'oeuvre? They are very nice.

MALE SPEAKER

Well, thanks.

MALE SPEAKER #2

Well, what did you think of the picture?

MALE SPEAKER

They should have saved it for Thanksgiving. What a turkey.

Undaunted, Esther goes to another group of people, again mincing and speaking in a ludicrous pseudo-upper-class accent.

ESTHER BLODGETT

Will you have some hors d'oeuvres, you do like hors d'oeuvres, don't you? I don't think there's anything so enjoyable as hors d'oeuvres before supper, and these are really delightful.

No response. She minces off. Male Guest #3, a dignified older man in black tie, looks after her uncomprehendingly.

Changing her act slightly, she puts one hand on her hip and approaches a third group with her mincing gait.

GUEST 1

And at the finish, the kid turns around and sings the lullaby to its mother.

ESTHER BLODGETT

(in a ghastly imitation of Mae West)

Pardon me, big boy, but would you like a little hors d'oeuvres? They say they're the best in town.

GUEST 1

(to Esther)

Don't tell me. I know, Mae West.

(To another guest)

That's a great twist. But where you going to find a two-months old baby that can sing?

In another scene in the house, Oliver Niles is descending a staircase, carrying a film script. Casey Burke comes up to him as he comes down.

CASEY BURKE

Hello, Oliver.

OLIVER NILES

Oh, hello, Casey.

CASEY BURKE

Do you want to fire me now, or wait until you see the picture? I'm not a director anymore, I'm a male nurse.

OLIVER NILES

What's the matter with the picture?

Oliver hands Casey the script.

CASEY BURKE

A guy by the name of Norman Maine. His work is beginning to interfere with his drinking.

Casey looks at the script.

CASEY BURKE

Oliver, don't tell me I'm to direct his next picture too?

OLIVER NILES

Mm-hmm.

CASEY BURKE

You were my favorite producer.

OLIVER NILES

Now wait a minute. You just go right on with your directing. I'll take care of these stars. I know how to handle them. I had a serious talk with Norman after that Hollywood Bowl occurrence. And you don't have to worry anymore about his behavior.

A butler comes up to them.

BUTLER

Excuse me, Mr. Niles. Mr. Libby of your publicity department is on the telephone. He says it's most important, sir. It's about Mr. Maine.

OLIVER NILES

Thank you. Oh, it's probably just some little thing.

CASEY BURKE

Mm-hmm. Of course, Oliver. I'll turn on the radio and see if they've called out the National Guard yet.

Oliver Niles sits down and takes the phone.

OLIVER NILES

Hello, Libby. What's the good word?

We now see Matt Libby in the press office.

MATT LIBBY

Mr. Norman Maine, America's Prince Charming, was apprehended driving an ambulance down Wilshire Boulevard with a siren going full blast. He explained he was a tree surgeon on a maternity case.

OLIVER NILES

Well, will it be in the papers?

MATT LIBBY

No, it won't be in the papers. But that's a nice expensive hobby of yours, keeping Mr. Maine's informal entertainments out of the public press.

OLIVER NILES

Oh, that's fine work, Libby. Try and see that no one gets to Norman. He's probably home sleeping it off.

Oliver Niles is startled to see Norman Maine coming from behind him on the staircase. He raps Oliver on the shoulder.

NORMAN MAINE

Oliver. Tsk, tsk. Why can't you forget those dopes at the studio for one night? Business, business, all the time. I don't know what's going to become of you.

Norman Maine enters the living room, where the party is still taking place. Anita comes up to him, and they hug.

ANITA REGIS

Norman, why didn't you call for me?

NORMAN MAINE

Well, my darling, why didn't I call for you?

ANITA REGIS

In case you'd forgotten, I was supposed to come here with you.

NORMAN MAINE

Oh, that! That's all right. I got here without any trouble.

ANITA REGIS

The only reason I don't slap your face. . .

NORMAN MAINE

Yes, yes, darling, I know.

He clutches at her wrist to make sure she does not slap him. John, an elderly guest in black tie, approaches them.

NORMAN MAINE

Hello, John.

JOHN

Oh, hello, Norman.

NORMAN MAINE

What's the matter with Oliver? He looks if he's had bad news.

Norman Maine goes over to Oliver Niles, who is at the bar.

NORMAN MAINE

What's the matter, old boy?

OLIVER NILES

Maybe I'm wrong. I guess I've been drinking too much
lately.

NORMAN MAINE

Oh, you have to cut it down. It's bad stuff. Scotch and
soda.

The bartender pours some Scotch in a glass and stops. Norman Maine urges him to pour out more.

NORMAN MAINE

Come on. Come on.

OLIVER NILES

The word, you know, is pronounced when.

NORMAN MAINE

Bad dialogue, Oliver.

OLIVER NILES

I'd rather not watch this.

Oliver Niles walks off.

NORMAN MAINE

You know best.

(to the bartender)

Soda.

The bartender proceeds to squirt seltzer into Norman Maine's
drink. Norman cuts him off after he has poured in only the
most minute amount.

NORMAN MAINE

Thank you.

He goes off, leaving the bartender looking perplexed.

We now see Norman Maine talking to Oliver Niles again.

NORMAN MAINE

Go ahead and say it. I've got it coming to me.

OLIVER NILES

Don't make it tougher on me, Norman. I don't want to stand here and preach, but take a look at my side of it. I'm trying to make pictures with you.

NORMAN MAINE

I know, I know. Costs are going up and the grosses are going down.

OLIVER NILES

No, it isn't that. I've made lots of money with you, and I can afford to take a loss, but I hate to see you going the way of so many others.

NORMAN MAINE

Why don't you get Lloyd's to insure you against me?

OLIVER NILES

You can't get insurance against a man forgetting who he is. You're a great star, Norman. But there's nobody so big that you can afford to have people refuse to work with him.

NORMAN MAINE

Who doesn't want to work with me?

OLIVER NILES

Shh, shh, quiet.

NORMAN MAINE

Listen, I know plenty of people who do.

OLIVER NILES

Yes. And so do I, but your real friends can't stand seeing you start to fall apart.

NORMAN MAINE

What do you mean by that?

OLIVER NILES

The first signs are always the same. Not being able to remember your lines. Cameraman struggling to cover your hangovers. And all because you have to have a good time, every day and every night. Listen, I've warned you for a long time.

NORMAN MAINE

Okay, Oliver, you're a swell guy. You won't lose any money on me, I promise you that. I'll be ready for the curtains when the time comes. When it does, here's my epitaph.

Norman Maine hands Oliver Niles a token that says, "Good for amusement only."

NORMAN MAINE

And now I think I'll have a little drink.

Norman Maine goes to the bar again.

NORMAN MAINE

Scotch and soda.

The bartender gapes at him, incredulous that he wants another drink so soon.

NORMAN MAINE

Scotch and soda.

The bartender pours a small amount.

NORMAN MAINE

Come on. Come on. Come on.

The bartender continues pouring. Finally, when the glass is almost full:

NORMAN MAINE

A little soda.

Esther Blodgett comes up to Norman Maine, still bearing her tray of hors d'oeuvre.

ESTHER BLODGETT

Caviar?

She is not trying any act at this point.

NORMAN MAINE

No, thank you.
>*(As she goes away, he calls her back).*
Yes? Pardon me.

Esther Blodgett comes back with the tray. He stares at her as he eats a canape.

ESTHER BLODGETT

Lovely. Lovely. No—I mean the caviar.

ESTHER BLODGETT

Mm-hmm.

NORMAN MAINE

No, don't go away. I'm starving. Really.

He looks down at her tray of caviar canapes, all of which are identical.

NORMAN MAINE

Which would you take?

ESTHER BLODGETT

I don't know.

NORMAN MAINE

You know, I don't know either. It's hard to choose. I think I'll take caviar.

Anita Regis approaches them haughtily.

ANITA REGIS

Mr. Maine doesn't care for any more. Do you, Normy?

NORMAN MAINE

No. Normy doesn't care for any more.

Esther goes off with the tray.

NORMAN MAINE

I think I shall get very drunk indeed.

He goes to the bar.

NORMAN MAINE

Scotch and soda.

He looks down and realizes that he still has a full glass.

                            NORMAN MAINE
                              (chuckling)

Sorry. I have some here.

In the kitchen, Esther is stacking plates. Norman Maine comes
in.

                          ESTHER BLODGETT

Oh.

                            NORMAN MAINE

Mind if I help?

He helpfully hands a plate to Esther. And then another.

                          ESTHER BLODGETT

Won't they miss you?

                            NORMAN MAINE

Oh, no, no. They'll just look under the table, and when
they see I'm not there, they'll forget the whole matter.
What's your name?

                          ESTHER BLODGETT

Esther Blodgett.

                            NORMAN MAINE

My name's Maine.

                          ESTHER BLODGETT

I know.

                            NORMAN MAINE

You do.

Esther giggles.

NORMAN MAINE

Huh? What's so funny?

ESTHER BLODGETT

I was just thinking about all your fans and how surprised they'd be to see you here helping me put plates away.

NORMAN MAINE

Oh, they, they don't know my finer side.

ESTHER BLODGETT

They'd be pretty envious of me meeting you this way in person.

NORMAN MAINE

Oh, how do you do? Well, tell me, are you disappointed?

ESTHER BLODGETT

Yes.

Norman drops a plate on the floor, and it smashes.

ESTHER BLODGETT

Now you've done it.

She continues to put plates away.

NORMAN MAINE

Oh, never mind that. That makes the room look lived in. Tell me, why are you disappointed?

ESTHER BLODGETT

I was sitting behind you at the Hollywood Bowl the night you didn't want to be photographed.

Norman Maine drops another plate.

NORMAN MAINE

Yeah. I'm told I crept into many a heart that night.

ESTHER BLODGETT

I can never explain this.

NORMAN MAINE

You know, you have very pretty hair.

ESTHER BLODGETT

You'd better get out of here.

NORMAN MAINE

And a sensitive mouth and a charming little. . .

Anita Regis comes in, haughty as usual.

ANITA REGIS

Precisely why are you here, instead of with the rest of the guests?

NORMAN MAINE

I'm just trying to be helpful.

ANITA REGIS

I see. Are you sure there's no other attraction?

NORMAN MAINE

Well, it might be that my old mania for putting plates away is coming back on me.

ANITA REGIS

It's rather odd. I always know where I can find you. If there's a pretty girl around.

NORMAN MAINE

It's not only odd, it's embarrassing.

ANITA REGIS

You're being deliberately insulting, Norman. I put up
with this long enough.

NORMAN MAINE

No, no, Anita, don't lose your temper. Remember, we
must try to keep the voice low. I know you'll excuse us
if we go on with our work?

Anita picks up large ceramic platter and smashes it over Norman's head. He falls down.

ANITA REGIS
(to Esther)

Now, see what you've done!

Anita storms out of the kitchen. Esther runs to the phone.
Norman beckons to her.

NORMAN MAINE

Come here, help me up.

ESTHER BLODGETT

Are you hurt?

NORMAN MAINE

No more than usual. Come on. The wolves are on us.
We have to get out of here.

ESTHER BLODGETT

Well, I can't. The dishes aren't finished.

NORMAN MAINE

Oh, yes they are.

He pushes the entire stack of plates onto the floor.

We now see Norman and Esther driving in Norman's open convertible. He pulls to a stop.

NORMAN MAINE

Well, I bet I know what you're going to say now.

ESTHER BLODGETT

What?

NORMAN MAINE

Good night.

ESTHER BLODGETT

Good night, and thanks.

NORMAN MAINE

Hey, wait a minute, wait a minute. You realize it that all I found out about you is that you are foolish enough to want to go into pictures.

ESTHER BLODGETT

Why is it foolish? Look at you.

NORMAN MAINE

Yeah, that's what I mean. No, I'd rather like to go into this matter a little more thoroughly.

ESTHER BLODGETT

Well, that's awfully nice of you.

NORMAN MAINE

But why don't we go on up to my place and talk it over?

ESTHER BLODGETT

Oh, no, thank you very much. But I really must say goodnight.

NORMAN MAINE

Goodnight.

ESTHER BLODGETT

But you are not angry?

NORMAN MAINE

No, no. I'm hungry.

ESTHER BLODGETT

Well, why don't you go and get something to eat?

NORMAN MAINE

Goodnight, Miss Blodgett.

ESTHER BLODGETT

Goodnight, Mr. Maine.

She walks off. Norman hurries after her.

NORMAN MAINE

Wait a minute. The least I can do is to see you to your door. Will I see you again?

ESTHER BLODGETT

I hope so.

NORMAN MAINE

Has anyone ever told you that you're lovely? Well, now you know.

ESTHER BLODGETT

Thank you.

NORMAN MAINE

This—it's hard to say, but I want to say it anyway. You know, on the screen, I'm a . . . you know . . . in private life, I mean, you know . . . but whatever I do, I still respect lovely things. And you're lovely. Do you understand?

ESTHER BLODGETT

Yes, I think I do.

NORMAN MAINE

And it isn't that bump on the head that's doing this.

ESTHER BLODGETT

I'm glad.

NORMAN MAINE

Goodnight.

ESTHER BLODGETT

Goodnight.

NORMAN MAINE

Hey, do you mind if I take one more look?

She smiles at him, and he smiles back. She goes inside.

The scene turns to Oliver Niles's bedroom, where he is sleeping. He is talking in his sleep.

OLIVER NILES

Go away. Quite impossible. I wouldn't even consider it. Oh, no, no. Hello.

(The phone rings; Niles picks it up.)

Who is it? Who? Norman! What have you done now? You're not in jail, are you? Oh, yes. I see. Oh, it's that again. I see. She's beautiful. Yeah, I know. You want me to give her a screen test? Yeah, certainly. She's got wonderful possibilities. Oh, you know she's got something. You knew all the other ones had something too.

We see Norman in his bed under the covers.

NORMAN MAINE

(on the phone)

Oh, no. I tell you, Oliver, she's got that sincerity and honestness and . . . sincerity and honestness that, that makes great actresses. Oliver, I am so sure of this girl that I want to take the test with her myself.

OLIVER NILES

Hmm.

NORMAN MAINE

Listen, Oliver, you've worked hard. You are entitled to a break. You get . . .

Norman intuits that Oliver is dozing off and whistles.

OLIVER NILES

Yes, I heard you. Anything. Anything. Yes. Yes. Yeah.

NORMAN MAINE

Oliver, look, you try to get a little steep now, old man. All right, boy. Good night.

Norman hangs up. Norman pulls off the bedcovers and stands up. He is still fully dressed in evening wear. He puts a champagne bottle on the bed in his place.

NORMAN MAINE

Now telephone book. Telephone book. Telephone.

He gropes around for the telephone book.

NORMAN MAINE

Hey, telephone. There you are!

The phone book is at the other end of the room. He staggers over to it and pages through it, half whistling and half singing. Still paging through it, he takes it to the bedside. He gets back into bed, nursing a champagne bottle like a teddy bear. He dials, muttering a number, then, confused, hangs up. He looks at the telephone book and finds that he has been reading it upside down. He turns it around and tears out a page.

Back at the Oleander Arms, Mr. Randall is shuffling through the upstairs hallway in his pajamas and a robe. He knocks on Esther's door.

ESTHER BLODGETT
(*still in her room*)

Yes.

MR. RANDALL

Telephone.

ESTHER BLODGETT

For me?

MR. RANDALL

Some drunk, trying to be funny. Says he's Norman Maine.

ESTHER BLODGETT

Oh, oh, oh. Thanks. I'll be right down.

And Miss Blodgett, would you give him a message for me? Tell him it's 3 o'clock in the morning!

Mr. Randall goes downstairs, followed by Esther. He opens up a folio containing a Racing Form, pulls it out grumpily, and goes upstairs. Esther picks up the phone.

ESTHER BLODGETT
(into the phone)

What? What? Oh! Oh, yes, yes, I'll be there. Oh, thank you!

Esther runs upstairs. We see Danny in his bed. Esther knocks and rushes in.

ESTHER BLODGETT

Danny!

DANIEL "DANNY" MCGUIRE

Huh?

ESTHER BLODGETT

Oh, Danny, what do you think? I'm going to take a test tomorrow, and Norman Maine's helping me do it.

DANIEL "DANNY" MCGUIRE

I'm taking one too. Garbo's assisting me.

Danny turns over and goes back to sleep. Esther runs out into the hallway and back into her room. Mr. Randall is still there. He is about to scold her, but he bumps into a light fixture hanging from the ceiling and smashes it. Mr. Randall whimpers and goes away.

We now see a piece of stationery: "Oliver Niles Productions. Tues., Feb. 4th. Call Sheet. Test #12,432. Director: Casey Burke. Set. Ext. Garden Set. Location: Stage #4."

The roster says, "Norman Maine: Time called: On-set, 9 a.m. Make-up: 8 a.m. Character, description, wardrobe: Boulevard Coat, Silk Hat. Esther Blodgett: 9 a.m., make-up 7 a.m. Dress as fitted."

On set, Casey Burke is directing, puffing his pipe. Esther is standing, somewhat uncomfortably dressed in a nineteenth-century dress. Casey is giving directions to the crew.

CASEY BURKE

Move that glow bulb in. Put a silk on that thorn. No. Is this right? Is this light too hot for you, Hattie? Okay. But put that on the back. Put a double on that 90. Bring it down a little. That's it. Pull down on that 150. Down on that 150. Leave me an Apple box.

Crew members bustle around Esther, pushing her around, including the costume lady, who makes a last-minute adjustment on her skirt. A makeup man approaches her with a perplexed look on his face. He examines her, shaping his hand into an imitation camera lens, and gazes through her at it. He then flicks something off her cheek and goes off. A man sprays insect repellant on the flowers of her hat, and for good measures, sprays a blast into the air. A crew man extends a tape toward her to measure her distance from the camera. Throughout this Esther looks baffled but excited.

CASEY BURKE

Listen, gentlemen, please, if you don't mind. This is just a test.

VARIOUS STAGE HANDS

Ready, Mr. Burke. Ready, Mr. Burke. Ready now. Mr. Burke. Mr. Burke, we're ready now. Mr. Burke, all ready?

Danny comes up to Casey Burke from behind and startles him by saying:

DANNY

We're ready, Mr. Burke.

Danny then shouts in a screeching voice:

DANNY

Quiet!

CASEY BURKE

All light, let's take it.

CREW MEMBERS

Quiet, quiet, quiet, quiet, quiet, quiet, quiet.

CASEY BURKE

Ready, Norman.

Norman emerges from his dressing van in full evening dress.

NORMAN MAINE

Yep.

CASEY BURKE

You ready, Miss . . . what's your name?

NORMAN MAINE

He'll soon know your name, Esther. The whole world's going to know it.

ESTHER BLODGETT

But I'm so scared. Maybe I better not try today.

NORMAN MAINE

Come on now, don't be foolish. They all had to go through this. Harlow. Lombard. Myrna Loy. And now Esther Blodgett.

ESTHER BLODGETT

All right, I'm ready.

CASEY BURKE

This is a take. Roll them. Quiet. Take.

We then see the bottom page of a contract being signed by both Oliver Niles and Esther Blodgett. The camera draws back, and we see that they are in Niles' office.

OLIVER NILES

I may as well tell you that my whole organization thinks I've gone a little nut to sign you. Well, maybe they're right. I've been nuts before. You see, all the experts seem to think that your type is a little mild for present-day taste. But I rather believe that tastes change, like eyebrows. And I think that also, like eyebrows, tastes are going back to the natural. You look like a nice girl. I think I'm going to like you. That's not important. I think the public will like you. That is important.

ESTHER BLODGETT

Yes. I see what you mean, I mean, I know it is.

OLIVER NILES

Well, you don't think it's going to be easy. Nothing you really want is ever given away free. You have to pay for it and usually with your heart.

ESTHER BLODGETT

Someone else told me that once.

OLIVER NILES

But you still have to work it out for yourself. Oh, well, all this is just a long way of saying, I'm glad you're with us and good luck to you. And now I'm going to turn you over to our demon press agent, Libby. Don't let him frighten you. He has a heart of gold, only harder. And for the love of Pete, learn to close your mouth and keep it closed, even in your love scenes.

As Esther leaves the office, she is greeted by Libby, who takes her away. Next we see them sitting in Libby's office, which is next to Niles's. Libby is in front of his typewriter.

MATT LIBBY

Are you a Russian?

ESTHER BLODGETT

No. I was born in Fillmore, North Dakota.

MATT LIBBY

Oh, no.

Libby begins typing.

MATT LIBBY

Saw light of day in a mountain cabin. A trapper's hut, high up in the Rockies. Go on.

ESTHER BLODGETT

Well, I always wanted to be an actress

MATT LIBBY

Dreamed of footlights as lonely kiddie. Are you sure there's no Russian in your family?

ESTHER BLODGETT

Positive.

MATT LIBBY

That's a shame. Well, what does your father do?

ESTHER BLODGETT

He's a farmer.

MATT LIBBY

Eh. Social registerite father, fed up with hypocrisies of 400, sought wilderness for consolation. There, amidst the mountain flowers, he raised another blossom, his lovely little daughter . . . what's your name?

ESTHER BLODGETT

Esther Victoria Blodgett.

Libby stands up and goes back into Niles's office.

OLIVER NILES

(dictating to a secretary)

Greatly appreciating your attention in this matter. Very truly . . .

MATT LIBBY

Do you know what her name is? Esther Victoria Blodgett.

OLIVER NILES

We will have to do something about that right away.

Esther is back in Niles's office, seated and looking uneasy. Libby is pacing around. The secretary is still there.

MATT LIBBY

Esther Victoria Blodgett.

OLIVER NILES

Well, that Blodgett is definitely out. Let's see. Esther Victoria. Victoria, Vicki. How about Vicki?

SECRETARY

Oh, I think that's terribly cute.

OLIVER NILES

Let's see. Vicki. Vicki? What?

MATT LIBBY

Vicki, Vicki, pronounced Vicki Vicki.

OLIVER NILES

Siesta, Besta, Dester. Festa.

MATT LIBBY

Oh, that's very pretty.

OLIVER NILES

Jester, Hester, Dester, Lester. Vicki Lester.

SECRETARY

Oh, I like that. Say it. Vicki Lester. Say it again. Vicki Lester.

OLIVER NILES

Say it again.

SECRETARY

Vicki Lester.

OLIVER NILES

Say it. Vicki Lester. Say Vicki Lester. Vicki Lester. Vicki Lester.

MATT LIBBY

Vicki Lester.

Oliver presses the intercom. Three aides come immediately into the office. In line, they recite.

MALE AIDE #1

Vicki Lester.

MALE AIDE #2

Vicki Lester.

FEMALE AIDE

Vicki Lester.

MATT LIBBY

Vicki Lester.

ESTHER BLODGETT

Vicki Lester.

We now see a radio broadcaster speaking on the air.

RADIO BROADCASTER

Oliver Niles Studio discovers new starlet, a Cinderella of the Rockies. Her name is Vicki Lester. Those who have peeked tell me she couldn't be di-voon. the face of an angel and such natural talents. Her voice is a symphony. Her very walk, they tell me, is enough to drive men mad.

Now we see Vicki walking onstage, with a posture coach directed her from a seat in the audience. Vicki walks in a very slow and careful but artificial step.

POSTURE COACH

Not that way. Get the lead out of your feet. Lift them up.

Vicki changes her walk.

POSTURE COACH

That's better. It's terrible, but it's better.

Now the scene shifts to Vicki with a speech coach.

VICKI LESTER

(reading)

The quality of mercy is not strained. It droppeth as the gentle rain from heaven.

SPEECH COACH

Speak through the mouth, my child, through the mouth. The nose is for smelling roses. Proceed.

We now see Vicki Lester being made up. She has several different brows drawn above eyes by a makeup assistant.

MAKEUP ARTIST

Does she have to look surprised all the time? Anyway, it's just a rough sketch.

MAKEUP ASSISTANT

Pretty small mouth, eh? Oh, well.

MAKEUP ARTIST

Give her that Crawford sneer.

The makeup assistant touches up her mouth a little.

MAKEUP ARTIST
This will give her that deep Dietrich mnyeh.

Another adjustment to her eyebrows.

MAKEUP ARTIST
We are on the wrong track. She still looks surprised.

A wide view of the commissary. A manager comes in and shouts to them all:

MANAGER
Listen up, drunk people, we're shooting on the set this morning, not in the commissary. So come on, snap into it.

Vicki Lester is at a table, rehearsing her lines.

VICKI LESTER
Acme Trucking Company. No, Mr. Smith is not in. Acme Trucking Company. No, Mr. Smith is not in.

At the commissary counter is Norman Maine, with actors in costume on stools alongside him, one dressed like an Indian chief. Waitress 1 comes up.

WAITRESS 1
Good morning. What can I bring you, Mr. Maine?

Waitress 2, a grey-haired woman, comes up from behind.

WAITRESS 2
(to Waitress 1)
That just shows how long you've been here.

Waitress 2 brings him a tray.

NORMAN MAINE

Mabel, bless you. How soon are you and I going to be married? Huh?

WAITRESS 2

I don't know. You'll have to ask my mother.

Norman takes his breakfast, a raw egg, and breaks it into a glass, salts it, and seasons it with Worcestershire sauce.

He overhears Vicki rehearsing her lines. She tries various voices and accents.

VICKI LESTER

Acme Trucking Company. No. Mr. Smythe is not in. Acme Trucking Company, Mr. Smith is not in. Acme! Naw, Smith ain't in. Acme Trucking Company. . .

Norman guzzles his raw egg and sits down next to Vicki.

VICKI LESTER

Acme Trucking Company. . .

NORMAN MAINE

Could I speak to Mr. Smith, please?

VICKI LESTER

Mr. Smith is not . . . Norman!

NORMAN MAINE

What's all this between you and Smith?

VICKI LESTER

I've got a part. It's only one line, but it's in the picture.

NORMAN MAINE

It's ambition that made you break that date with me last night.

VICKI LESTER

Well, I had to be here so early this morning, and . . .

NORMAN MAINE

So did I. I had to stay up all night to make it.

VICKI LESTER

You started your picture, haven't you?

NORMAN MAINE

No. No. We're still in a testing stage. We can't seem to get the right girl for the lead.

VICKI LESTER

Gee. You think with all the girls there are that . . .

NORMAN MAINE

Yeah, but this one's got to be different. She's got to be little and cute and sweet and intelligent—well, blow me down!

VICKI LESTER

What?

NORMAN MAINE

Well, close my tired old eyes.

VICKI LESTER

What is it?

NORMAN MAINE

Hold everything. Come on. Come on.

Norman grabs her and rushes her out of the commissary.

Norman and Vicki are back in Oliver's office.

NORMAN MAINE

You've been through the whole casting directory.

VICKI LESTER

I'll work day and night, Mr. Niles.

NORMAN MAINE

And I'll work with her, Oliver.

VICKI LESTER

And I can be mean or nasty or anything you want, Mr. Niles.

NORMAN MAINE

If she clicks, Oliver, you've got a star overnight.

OLIVER NILES

Okay.

Oliver and Norman shake hands.

We now see an announcement on a film screen: "You are about to see the Preview of a picture that has not been finally edited. Your opinion will be appreciated. Please mail comment cards."

Then, the opening credits: "Oliver Niles presents Norman Maine in 'The Enchanted Hour.'" Fanfare and applause. Then: "introducing Vicki Lester."

The camera zeros in on Norman and Vicki watching in the audience. They hear the applause.

Wait until you hear them at the end of the picture!

He takes her hand and gently crosses her fingers, then brings his own finger to his lips.

We now see the film. First, a screen that says, "When the world tripped politely to the genteel music of spinnets."

Then a drawing room, where Vicki, dressed in Regency style, comes in. She is followed by Norman, in the masculine dress of the same period.

VICKI LESTER

(in character)

Do you think we were noticed?

NORMAN MAINE

(in character)

By no one. They're much too busy playing at croquet. I've loved you all my life.

VICKI LESTER

But we only met two days ago.

NORMAN MAINE

That's when my life began.

They kiss onscreen. In the audience, Norman grasps Vicki by the arm. She nestles into his shoulder.

The scene changes to the outside of a movie theater, which says on the marquee, "Preview Tonite." Oliver comes outside and stands off to catch the comments from the audience as they come out.

FEMALE MOVIE GOER 1

Ain't she cute! You know, I think she's the same type
I am, don't you?

FEMALE MOVIE GOER 2

I think she's sweet.

MALE MOVIE GOER 1

Well, it's Vicki Lester's picture, all right.

FEMALE MOVIE GOER 3

I think she was much better than he was.

FEMALE MOVIE GOER 4

These producers are so horribly dumb. They won't
know how good she is.

MALE MOVIE GOER 2

Well, maybe it's because she's a good girl.

MALE MOVIE GOER 3

Well, I mean, Norman's not so bad, but it's Vicki Lester
they'll go to see.

FEMALE MOVIE GOER 5

Isn't she a darling?

FEMALE MOVIE GOER 6

I think she's the most precious little thing I've ever
seen.

Libby and two reviewers are standing aside, talking.

REVIEWER 1

She's a knockout, Libby.

MATT LIBBY

You might mention that when you write your review.

REVIEWER 1

That Lester kid's a gold mine.

MATT LIBBY

Didn't you like Norman Maine?

REPORTER 2

Was he in it?

The reporters chuckle and go off.

CASEY BURKE

Libby, I'm afraid we have another hit.

MATT LIBBY

It's in the bag, neatly tied up with beautiful pink ribbons.

OLIVER NILES

Hey, where Norman and Vicki?

MATT LIBBY

I don't know. I thought you had them.

OLIVER NILES

I wish they'd come. We're having a party at the Trocadero.

Now Norman and Vicki are emerging from an emergency exit of the theater.

VICKI LESTER

Isn't it thrilling running away from people? Norman, it's so exciting, so . . .

NORMAN MAINE

So new. A star is born. Come on, come.

Outside, we see limousines arriving in front of the Café Trocadero.

The scene switches. Norman and Vicki are standing on a balcony, surveying the night expanse of Los Angeles.

VICKI LESTER

It is wonderful, isn't it? A crazy quilt.

NORMAN MAINE

Well, it's a carpet that spread for you. It's all yours from now on, you know. It's coming you're a success. You have everything in the world you want. I hope it'll make you happy.

VICKI LESTER

Hasn't it you?

NORMAN MAINE

No. But there was one thing I never had. Lots of times I told myself I'd found it, but I always knew I was lying. Still, I never stopped looking for it.

VICKI LESTER

Maybe it'll come.

NORMAN MAINE

Well, I think it has come, Esther. I only wish it weren't too late.

VICKI LESTER

Oh, but it's not too late.

NORMAN MAINE

Oh, you can't throw away your life the way I've thrown away mine and have anything left that's good enough, no.

VICKI LESTER

You can, Noman, you can.

NORMAN MAINE

You mustn't tell me that, Esther. I'm so afraid that I'll believe it.

Esther nuzzles up against him.

We are now watching a fight. Norman and Vicki are in the audience. One fighter is getting the better of the other.

NORMAN MAINE
(to a fighter)

Come on, Garcia. shoot out your right! Swell, isn't it?

VICKI LESTER

This is lovely.

NORMAN MAINE

Watch Garcia again.
(to the fighter)

Can't you hear me, Garcia? Shoot your right!

One fighter, Garcia, has the other on the ropes. He hits him repeatedly, and the other fighter falls.

NORMAN MAINE

He's got him!

VICKI LESTER

He did, didn't he?

NORMAN MAINE

Yeah, but he'll be up, though. You like it?

The scene goes back to the boxers. Garcia hits the other fighter repeatedly. Now back to Norman and Vicki.

VICKI LESTER

Yeah, I do.

NORMAN MAINE

You like me?

VICKI LESTER

Yeah, I do.

NORMAN MAINE

That reminds me. Will you marry me?

VICKI LESTER

No. Thank you.

NORMAN MAINE

Come on. Garcia, you finish him!

(to Vicki)

Why won't you marry me?

VICKI LESTER

Because you're not dependable.

NORMAN MAINE

Hey, shoot your right!

VICKI LESTER

You throw away your money.

NORMAN MAINE

Break him up in there. Break him up.

VICKI LESTER

And you drink so much.

NORMAN MAINE

Well, suppose I quit drinking.

VICKI LESTER

Yes.

NORMAN MAINE

Come on. Garcia, shoot the right in there, the right.

(to Vicki)

Suppose I saved my money?

VICKI LESTER

Yes.

NORMAN MAINE

(to Garcia)

There you go! Let him have it!

(to Vicki)

Suppose I became absolutely dependable on all occasions.

VICKI LESTER

Yes.

Garcia and the other fighter are down, but Garcia gets up. The referee holds up Garcia's hand, indicating that he has won.

NORMAN MAINE

Hey, Garcia, he's got him, he's got him.

VICKI LESTER

He certainly did.

Long shot of the boxing ring. Fanfare. The lights of photographers flashing.

Norman and Vicki go out with the audience.

NORMAN MAINE

Gee, that was a beautiful fight.

VICKI LESTER

Norman?

NORMAN MAINE

Yes?

Vicki Lester

You'd do all that if I said I'd marry you?

NORMAN MAINE

No, certainly not. I was just supposing.

Now Norman and Vicki are in Oliver's office.

NORMAN MAINE

We are going to be married. Guess I didn't read that line right. I'll try it again.

(with exaggerated distinction)

We—are—going—to be married.

VICKI LESTER

Both of us.

NORMAN MAINE

Yeah. To each other. What do you think of that?

OLIVER NILES

When, where?

NORMAN MAINE

Well, we thought we'd elope in the conventional manner.

Oliver looks downcast.

VICKI LESTER

What's the matter?

NORMAN MAINE

He's trying to decide whether it's good for the studio.

VICKI LESTER

Is it?

OLIVER NILES

It is. And bless you, my children. When's it going to happen?

NORMAN MAINE

Oh, we thought we'd just sneak out sometime.

VICKI LESTER

We're not telling anyone but you.

Matt Libby dashes into the office with a sheet of paper.

MATT LIBBY

Listen to this. The screen's ideal romance blossomed into breathtaking reality today when Vicki Lester and Norman Maine, America's dream lovers, slipped quietly through the portals of holy matrimony. How does it sound?

NORMAN MAINE

Horrible.

VICKI LESTER

But you see, we are going to elope.

MATT LIBBY

Sure, you are. It'll be the biggest elopement this town ever saw. We'll get a tie-up with the army. Have you escorted all the way down to Yuma by 20 of their new bombing planes.

VICKI LESTER

(to Norman)

Is he going with us?

MATT LIBBY

(to Oliver)

Don't you think we can work this thing out better alone? No sense in bothering the happy couple with all the details. I'll see to it that you get a carbon copy of the whole layout.

NORMAN MAINE

I can hardly wait. I'm sorry. We didn't realize that we were in the way. While you're settling the details, you don't mind if I take this woman out and buy her a ring?

MATT LIBBY

Sure, go ahead. We want everything legal.

They go out.

MATT LIBBY

That's a charming match. A nice girl like Vicki and public nuisance number one.

OLIVER NILES

Oh, wait a minute, Libby, Norman's all right. And if you'll pardon my pointing, Vicki's business is her own. It doesn't require any comments.

MATT LIBBY

I wasn't making any comments. I just said it was a rotten shame.

OLIVER NILES

Now go ahead and plan the elopement.

MATT LIBBY

Oh, that elopement stuff is out. You can't get any scope in that. We're going to have a wedding. Where will we have it?

OLIVER NILES

Customary place, I believe, is a church.

MATT LIBBY

Nah, it's been done. This has got to be something big. The beach. I can visualize it. The bridesmaids in bathing suits. 20,000 Santa Monica schoolchildren spelling out the word "love." It's a novelty, but is it big enough? Why not the city hall? A police escort of every motorcycle cop in town, sirens, screaming, confetti pouring out of buildings like the Lindberg reception in New York, only on a big scale.

Oliver looks at Libby distastefully.

LIBBY

What's the matter? Isn't it big enough?

We are now in a courthouse. Two inmates are staring through the bars.

JUSTICE OF THE PEACE
(offscreen)

And now, if any man can show just cause why these two may not be lawfully joined together, let him now speak or else hereafter forever, hold his peace. Do you, Alfred Hinkel, take this woman as your lawful wedded wife?

The camera pulls back to reveal Norman and Vicki standing in front of the justice of the peace.

JUSTICE OF THE PEACE

Will you love comfort, and keep her in sickness and health, as long as you both shall live?

ALFRED HINKEL

I will.

JUSTICE OF THE PEACE

Will you—beg your pardon. Will you, Esther Blodgett, take this man as your lawful wedded husband. Will you obey, serve, love, honor, and keep him in sickness and heath, as long as you both shall live?

ESTHER BLODGETT

I will.

JUSTICE OF THE PEACE

Place the ring on her finger. Hurry, please.

The camera pulls back to reveal Danny, who is standing as witness.

JUSTICE OF THE PEACE

Now, by virtues of the power invested in me as justice of the peace of San Bardo Township, County of Los Angeles, I pronounce you man and wife.

The couple kiss. The men behind bars applaud.

DANIEL "DANNY" MCGUIRE

Quiet!

JUSTICE OF THE PEACE

And now I must exercise my prerogative of office.

The justice kisses the bride on the cheek.

JUSTICE OF THE PEACE

I hope you'll be very happy. Mrs. Hinkel.

ESTHER HINKEL

Thank you.

ALFRED HINKEL

Thank you, sir. Thank you very much.

JUSTICE OF THE PEACE

Now if you'll please sign the license.

DANIEL "DANNY" MCGUIRE

Oh, oh, yeah.

JUSTICE OF THE PEACE

You know, Mrs. Hinkel, I can't help but believe I've seen you somewhere before.

ESTHER HINKEL

Oh, really? Well I believe this is the first time I've ever been in San Bardo.

JUSTICE OF THE PEACE

You know, your face is familiar too, Mr. Hinkel . . .

ALFRED HENKE

(interrupting)

Thank you very much.

DANIEL "DANNY MCGUIRE

Here's your receipt.

ALFRED HINKEL

Thank you. Goodbye.

ESTHER HINKEL

Goodbye.

JUSTICE OF THE PEACE

See you.

ALFRED HINKEL

See you again. Goodbye.

Outside the courtroom:

DANIEL "DANNY" MCGUIRE

Yeah. I think we got by with it.

NORMAN MAINE

But it was close that JP was just beginning to remember where he'd seen us.

ESTHER HINKEL

Well, anyway, we got away from Libby.

They are now coming out of the municipal building. Libby comes up to them.

MATT LIBBY

Hello, Toots. If you will be kind enough to glance between my shoulder blades, Mr. and Mrs. Hinkel, you'll find there a knife buried to the hilt. On the handle are your initials.

NORMAN MAINE

Very good seeing you.

(to Danny)

Hold him, Danny.

Danny holds back Libby while the two dash into and drive off in Norman's convertible.

MATT LIBBY

There goes a couple of rats I raised from mice.

DANIEL "DANNY" MCGUIRE

Well, they got a right to get married, haven't they?

MATT LIBBY

They haven't got any right to double-cross the public, and they haven't done it yet!

Libby runs into the building.

DANIEL "DANNY" MCGUIRE

Hey!

Danny follows him.

Libby rushes into a courtroom, where a trial is being held. A bailiff is reading charges.

BAILIFF

People versus Porky Washington, who is charged with violating Section 600 . . .

Libby grabs the phone from the judge's desk.

JUDGE

Young man, you are in contempt of court.

MATT LIBBY

Operator, get me the Los Angeles Tribune.

JUDGE

I have a good mind to put you under arrest.

MATT LIBBY

Wait until I make this call.

(to the bailiff)

You wait too. Tribune, give me the city desk. Johnny, this is Matt Libby. I got a flash for you. Norman Maine and Vicki Lester were married at 230 this afternoon.

JUDGE

Vicki Lester! Court recessed!

The judge slams down the gavel. The judge and court attendees dash madly out of the office.

The front page of a tabloid is displayed:

Vicki Loves in Trailer!

Next we see a long shot of a car pulling a trailer along a winding road in a desert landscape. We see Norman at the wheel, whistling. In the inside of the trailer, Vicky is singing, cooking a steak:

ESTHER HINKEL
Whoa, give me a horse, a great big horse, a great big buckaroo, and let me wahoo, wahoo, wahoo! . . .

There is a lurch inside the trailer, knocking the steak onto the floor.

VICK LESTER
Wahoo.

Outside, the car drives off the road and lurches to a halt, stuck. Norman revs up the engine, but it does no good. The engine makes an alarming grinding noise, and he turns it off.

Inside the trailer, Esther is picking up the steak, which has fallen to the floor. Norman comes in.

ESTHER HINKEL
Wahoo.

NORMAN MAINE
Hey, wahoo. I don't want to sound immodest, but I think I've stripped the gear.

ESTHER HINKEL

Well, sit down, won't you, and let's get acquainted. We'll probably be seeing quite a bit of each other from now on.

NORMAN MAINE

Yep. Might just as well break the ice now as later.

(He kisses her.)

Now we're old friends. So have I got time for a shower before dinner?

ESTHER HINKEL

Plenty, if you can find the shower.

NORMAN MAINE

I never can remember where that thing is. Does it pull out or slide under?

ESTHER HINKEL

Here, I think I can find it. No, that's the linen closet. Here it is.

NORMAN MAINE

Nice work.

ESTHER HINKEL

Oh, half the time those things are just luck. Now I'll see if I can disinfect this steak.

She brushes off the steak and pumps water onto it to wash it off.

NORMAN MAINE

(coming out of the shower)

Esther, there's no soap.

ESTHER HINKEL

Here.

She hands him a bar from the kitchen sink.

NORMAN MAINE

Thank you. Oh, and Esther . . .

ESTHER HINKEL

Yes, dear.

NORMAN MAINE

I'll need a washcloth.

She hands him a washcloth.

ESTHER HINKEL

How are you fixed for cigarettes?

NORMAN MAINE

You know, I never smoke under water.

They kiss.

NORMAN
(in the shower)

What, what do I do to make this thing work?

ESTHER HINKEL

Pull that gadget at the top and pray for rain.

NORMAN MAINE

Well, I can't reach it. I can't get my hands up there.

ESTHER HINKEL

If you've gone in there with your arms down, you'll never get your bath, unless you're a contortionist.

NORMAN MAINE

Yeah. Well, I'm not a contortionist, and don't throw that up to me now. You knew it when you married me. Can you close this door, please?

Esther closes the door.

NORMAN MAINE

Thank you.

In the shower, Norman pulls the plug and is drenched in a cascade of water.

NORMAN

Help, help!

ESTHER HINKEL

Norman. Norman. Here comes a car.

NORMAN MAINE

You got to—huh?

ESTHER HINKEL

Here, quick.

NORMAN MAINE

Quick, what?

She puts a bathrobe around him.

ESTHER HINKEL

Quick. Go out and stop them and ask for help.

NORMAN MAINE

Oh, I'll catch cold.

ESTHER HINKEL

Oh, you'll get warm again.

NORMAN MAINE

Yeah, what do I do if they recognize me?

ESTHER HINKEL

Now you have you keep your face down. Go on. There may not be another car for a week.

NORMAN MAINE

All right.

Judd Baker pulls up in a jalopy and stops.

JUDD BAKER

Howdy, Partner.

NORMAN MAINE

Howdy.

JUDD BAKER

Stuck?

NORMAN MAINE

Yeah. How'd you guess it? Can you get us some help?

JUDD BAKER

Well, I reckon not. You know, it's a long way to town. We're pretty busy down at the place.

NORMAN MAINE

Well, I have to get out of here. I've got my wife with me.

JUDD BAKER

Don't she like the country?

• 76 •

NORMAN MAINE

No. No. And we're short of food.

JUDD BAKER

There's a lot of game in them woods.

NORMAN MAINE

No. My wife can't shoot.

JUDD BAKER

Well, you're sure up against it. Sorry, I can't do anything for you.

NORMAN MAINE

Well, wait, listen, I, I'll be frank with you. I'm Norman Maine.

JUDD BAKER

Who?

NORMAN MAINE

Norman Maine!

JUDD BAKER

Well, my name is Judd Baker. Glad to have met you. Well, so long.

He drives off.

NORMAN MAINE

Hey, wait a minute! Listen, you don't—!

ESTHER HINKEL

So you're Norman Maine.

The screen shows a shot of a gossip column by one Artie Garver which says, "What famous male star has stopped gargling the grog and is now taking a non-alcoholic honeymoon? But why do friends think his bride came about six performances too late as far as the public is concerned?"

In Oliver Niles' office, Matt Libby is complaining.

MATT LIBBY

I got my prestige to look out for. I'm supposed to be the best publicity man in the racket, and they laugh themselves sick when I even try to get a decent mention of Maine.

OLIVER NILES

Yes, I know how sensitive you are, Libby. And I don't like to see your feelings hurt.

MATT LIBBY

Thanks, Boss. Now Vicki, there's a dish for free space. But if Maine swam across the Pacific, the papers would keep it a secret. Well, the exhibitors don't like him, the critics don't like him, the public don't like him, and I don't like him. Who likes him?

Now we see Maine and Esther jogging across the lawn of a mansion toward a pond.

ESTHER HINKEL

Oh, but darling, this is almost too much of a surprise. And there I was in my touching innocence, thinking we were going to live at the beach house.

NORMAN MAINE

Oh, we'll still keep the place at Malibu, but this is special. This is our castle. It used to be in the air, you know. We'll never use any ugly words like contracts and pictures and careers. When we come in those gates, we check the studio outside. Come on, I got another little surprise for you.

They skip past the pond, with its white swans, and arrive at a swimming pool.

ESTHER HINKEL

Oh, Noman. It's lovely.

NORMAN MAINE

So are you lovely! The whole world's lovely.

Libby marches up with a photographer in tow.

MATT LIBBY

Hey, hold it.

The couple embraces with embarrassment. The photographer snaps a picture.

MATT LIBBY

That's it. Caption their honeymoon never ends. All right, let's get some pictures. Now, if the bride will sit here and the groom stand behind her, we'll have something unique.

Norman and Esther obey him. Oliver Niles approaches from behind. Norman sees him, but Libby does not.

Now let's go after something different. You sit down, and she'll stand up.

The couple exchange places.

Pretty radical, isn't it?

Yeah, but in a nice way. Okay, Otto, fire. Caption their honeymoon begins anew.

Oliver Niles comes up to them.

Ah, the producer. Caption their honeymoon ceases abruptly. Hello, Oliver. Glad to see you.

Oh, I'm glad you're back.

Thank you.

Vicki, how well you're looking.

Hello, Oliver.

Am I interrupting?

Yes. Thank you.

MATT LIBBY

Just want a couple more pictures.

OTTO

That's enough for both of them. What they're asking for is exclusives of Miss Lester, alone.

NORMAN MAINE

Oh, I see. Well, come on, Oliver, let you and me get exclusive.

OLIVER NILES

See you later, Vicki.

Norman and Oliver move off.

NORMAN MAINE

But don't worry, Otto, my camera smashing days are over.

OTTO
(muttering)

Those ain't your only days are over. Oh, hold that, Ms. Lester.

The photographer takes a picture of her.

MATT LIBBY

Gorgeous.

Norman and Oliver sit down at a poolside table.

NORMAN MAINE

Well, Oliver, how's the dividend situation?

OLIVER NILES

Very pleasant. I think we'll show 2 million in the next quarter.

NORMAN NILES

Oh, God. Smart move of mine to sell my stock, eh? Oh, well, when you need money, you need it.

OLIVER NILES

Some people save up for just such an event. You know, there's bound to be a rainy day occasionally.

NORMAN MAINE

Yeah. But as a citizen of California, I've always refused to admit that.

OLIVER NILES

Yes, I know, but still it does rain.

NORMAN MAINE

Well, anyway, you can thank me for some of those dividends of yours.

OLIVER NILES
(lighting a cigarette)

Mm-hmm.

NORMAN MAINE

Oh, can't you?

OLIVER NILES

Oh, sure, sure.

NORMAN MAINE

That was a little too quick, Oliver. The Enchanted Hour was a smash hit, wasn't it?

OLIVER NILES

Well, it made Vicki a star overnight.

NORMAN MAINE

As it should have. What about me?

OLIVER NILES

Well, let's talk about business at the office, Norman. Beautiful pool you have here, beautiful.

NORMAN MAINE

Oh, no, let's talk about it here. Didn't they like me?

OLIVER NILES

Well, maybe the part wasn't just right.

NORMAN MAINE

It was the best part of the year. Look, Oliver, you think I'm slipping?

OLIVER NILES

Can you take it?

NORMAN MAINE

Yeah, go ahead.

OLIVER NILES

The tense is wrong. You're not slipping; you've slipped.

NORMAN MAINE

Well, well, my fan mail's still big.

OLIVER NILES

Norman, Norman. Fans will write to anybody for a photograph. It only costs 3 cents for a stamp. And that makes photographs cheaper than wallpaper. But every 25 cents they pay for a theater ticket buys them the right to be a critic. And your last few performances, Norman, have not pleased your critics.

NORMAN MAINE

You remember I told you I'd be ready for the curtains when the time came? Here it is. Let's call off the contract. No hard feelings.

OLIVER NILES

We're not quitting, either of us. There's no explaining these things. We've all seen how the public turns. Maybe we can turn them back. I've got a swell script lined up for you

NORMAN MAINE

About Esther . . . if you think that I'm going to get in her way . . .

OLIVER NILES

Well, as a matter of fact, as it happens, there's no part in this story for her. I'd more or less planned to star her in a picture of her own, with that young Pemberton opposite her. He's coming along nicely.

NORMAN MAINE

Good for young Pemberton. All right, Oliver. We'll make a try at it. Let's hope it's not too late.

A workman is pasting over a billboard that said, "Norman Maine in The Enchanted Hour" to make it say, "Vicki Lester in The Enchanted Hour."

Now the screen displays the front cover of a prospectus that says, "Mr. Exhibitor, here's a message of vital importance for you. Get rich with Oliver Niles Productions."

A cigar-chomping exhibitor goes through it. He turns over the first page, which reads, "Productions starring Vicki Lester, the screen's latest sensation."

EXHIBITOR

No argument. I'll buy those.

He turns the page again to see a page that says, "Productions starring Norman Maine, the screen's most finished actor."

EXHIBITOR

Hah! "The screen's most finished actor." I'll say he's finished. He keeps them away in droves.

In the studio mailroom, a mail assistant flings some letters into a pigeonhole marked, "Norman Maine." It is half full. Next to it is a pigeonhole labeled, "Vicki Lester." It is jammed.

Next we see the front page of Theatre Men's Guide, with the headline, "Norman Maine Contract with Niles Cancelled." The camera zeroes in on a subhead: "Theatre men who were short-sighted enough to buy the Norman Maine pictures on this year's Oliver Niles Schedule will be glad that they will be released from this burden on them and their audiences. Niles has finally bought off the Maine contract for an unknown figure . . . Orchids to Niles!"

We see a long night shot of the Malibu shore in front of the Maine house, where a sole light is burning through a window.

Inside, Norman Maine is practicing his putting. The phone rings, and he rushes to it and answers.

NORMAN MAINE

Hello? No, no, Miss Lester isn't home as yet. No, I'm not the butler, but I can take a message just as well as he can, honest.

We now see Artie Carver, gossip columnist, on the other end of the line.

ARTIE CARVER

Oh, is that you, Norman? Swell. Listen, Norman, this is Artie Carver. How are ya, kid? Swell. Say I hear you through with Oliver Niles. Is that on the level?

NORMAN MAINE

Oh, please, Artie. I'm not news anymore. Forget it.

ARTIE CARVER

Say, what kind of a settlement did you make on your contract? Give me a figure so I can do a story on it.

NORMAN MAINE

There was no money involved; we just called it quits.

ARTIE CARVER

Okay. Okay. I'll fill in my own figure. Say, by the way, I've been trying to get an interview with Vicki for two weeks, but she's always busy. How about you giving an old pal a break by speaking to her for me?

NORMAN MAINE

Sure. I'll ask her.

ARTIE CARVER

Swell! So long.

Artie hangs up. Vicki comes into the Maine living room, wearing an eighteenth-century costume, and she and Norman embrace ardently.

VICKI LESTER

I didn't mean to be late, darling, but Casey wanted me . . .

NORMAN MAINE

All right. You're here now.

VICKI LESTER

What's new today?

NORMAN MAINE

Nothing. Haven't been out of the house.

VICKI LESTER

Let's go somewhere tonight.

NORMAN MAINE

No, no. You're tired. We'll stay in.

VICKI LESTER

I'm not tired, really.

NORMAN MAINE

Oh, yes you are. You've got a hard day ahead of you. Anyway, I see so little of you. I'd like to have you to myself.

VICKI LESTER

Oh, but it's the servants' night out. We haven't any . . .

NORMAN MAINE

Yes, we have. I fixed a little snack with my own lily-white hands. I'm learning to cook in my spare time.

VICKI LESTER

Thanks. I think I'll marry you.

NORMAN MAINE

I get it. You want to make an honest cook of me. Comes in on wheels in this joint. Hang on.

He goes out. Vicki sitting at a mirror, removes her cap, frizzes her hair with delight, and starts to brush it. Norman comes in, wheeling in a table.

NORMAN MAINE

There. How does it look?

She turns around and sees an elegant setting for two.

VICKI LESTER

Wonderful.

He wheels it over in front of two chairs, and they sit down.

NORMAN MAINE

Ah, that's what I thought. Now then, don't be formal. Just pitch in. There you are.

He hands her a plate of enormously thick sandwiches. She takes one and tries to eat, but cannot fit it in her mouth. There is a huge glass of milk on the table.

VICKI LESTER

I'm afraid my mouth's not quite big enough.

NORMAN MAINE

I'll measure it next time and make them to size.

VICKI LESTER

A little hard to lift too.

NORMAN MAINE

In fact, I think I'll take those measurements right now.

He goes over and kisses her.

NORMAN MAINE

And that's what I wait for all day.

VICKI LESTER

That's why I rush home without even changing my costume.

NORMAN MAINE

We're forgetting that we're hungry. Like a sandwich?

VICKI LESTER

Thank you. I still have a little work on this one.

Norman sits down opposite her, takes his glass of milk, raises it in something of a toast, and drinks from it.

VICKI LESTER

Norman, will you unhook my dress? I can't breathe.

He helps her unhook her dress.

NORMAN MAINE

Mm-Hmm. You know, all the time I thought it was the kiss that made you breathless. A lot of hooks, huh? Why don't you have a zipper?

VICKI LESTER

That's a good idea.

NORMAN MAINE

Feel better?

VICKI LESTER

Yes!

He hugs and kisses her again. They both gaze into a mirror.

NORMAN MAINE

Oh, don't look now, but I think that guy on your left is
in love with you.

VICKI LESTER

I hope so.

They kiss. The doorbell rings repeatedly.

NORMAN MAINE

It's the doorbell.

VICKI LESTER

Is it? Maybe they'll go away.

NORMAN MAINE

Oh, they never do at a time like this. Just a minute,
dear, I'll be right back.

He goes over and answers the door. A mailman is holding a
package.

MAILMAN

Does Vicki Lester live here?

NORMAN MAINE

Yes.

MAILMAN

I got a package for her.

NORMAN MAINE

I'll sign for it.

MAILMAN

Who are you?

NORMAN MAINE

I'm her husband.

MAILMAN

Oh, sure. Sign right here, Mr. Lester.

Norman looks at him, startled and hurt. The mailman senses that he has said something wrong. Norman signs for the package, and closes the door on the mailman, who still does not understand what is wrong.

Norman brings the package over to Vicki, who is still sitting at the table.

NORMAN MAINE

A package for you. And by the way, I forgot to tell you, they want you for a benefit, the Shrine Auditorium, next Wednesday night. I told them I'd ask you, and . . .

VICKI LESTER

Oh, darling, I don't want to hear about that now.

NORMAN MAINE

Well, you'd better wait until I finish before I forget them all. The Academy Dinner secretary phoned. She wants to know if you want a table reserved for you. Oh, yes. Artie Carver called and asked if I'd use my influence with you to get him an interview. I told him I'd try. That was all, I think.

VICKI LESTER

Oh, Norman, let's don't talk about those things now. We are forgetting the wonderful food you prepared.

NORMAN MAINE

Well, I'm not very hungry now. I think I'll fix me a little drink.

He goes off.

VICKI LESTER

But Norman!

The screen shows invitations: "Academy of Motion Picture Arts and Sciences Eighth Annual Awards of Merit Banquet in the Biltmore Bowl, Biltmore Hotel."

Then we see the banquet. The room is filled with people in evening dress. We hear applause.

Vicki and Oliver are sitting at a table.

VICKI LESTER

I wish Norman would come.

OLIVER NILES

Stop worrying and think how nice that statue is going to look on your mantelpiece.

VICKI LESTER

Do you suppose anything's happened to him?

OLIVER NILES

But of course not. He's just been held up in traffic. You think about that statuette.

ANNOUNCER

And now we arrive at the climax of the annual dinner of the Academy of Motion Picture Arts and Sciences. The highest award within our power to bestow. We have already applauded with our hearts as well as our hands while awards have been given those gentlemen who during the past year have rendered distinguished service to the motion picture industry. We now pay honor to the ladies, or rather to one lady. We offer to her the Academy Award for the finest performance of the past year. She has already had the world's acclaim, but this is the tribute of our fellow workers, the men and women of this industry. It is not only my pleasure but my privilege to present this award to the actress who created the unforgettable Anna in Dream without End. Miss Vicki Lester.

[Applause]

Vicki rises and goes to the podium, accompanied partway by Oliver.

ANNOUNCER

What more can we say, Miss Lester? This says it all for us.

[Applause]

She beams but looks uneasily around for Norman.

VICKI LESTER

Ladies and gentlemen. When something like this happens to you and you try to tell how you feel about it, you find that out of all the words in the world, there are only two that really mean anything. Thank you. All I can do is to say them to you from my heart. All I can do is to keep on saying them.

Norman barges into the ballroom, applauding loudly, drunk.

NORMAN MAINE

Hurray! That's fine. That's a very pretty speech, my dear, very pretty. You said the right thing. I want to be the very first one to congratulate you on that valuable little piece of bric-a-brac.

Norman comes to her on the podium, clasps her hand, making her drop the Oscar.

NORMAN MAINE

Now I want to make a speech. Gentlemen of the Academy and fellow suckers, I got one of those once for a best performance. They don't mean a thing. People get them every year. What I want is a special award, something nobody else can get. I want a statue for the worst performance of the year. In fact, I want three statues for the three worst performances of the year, because I've earned them. And every single one of you that saw those last masterpieces of mine knows that I've earned them.

OLIVER NILES

Libby, start the music.

NORMAN MAINE

What I'm here to find out is, do I get them, or do I get them? Answer yes or no.

Vicki goes up to him. He swings his arms out, accidentally hitting her in the face. She looks at him compassionately and takes him by the arm. He looks at her with remorse. He kisses her as they take their seats.

VICKI LESTER

Norman, my darling, let's go and sit down.

OLIVER NILES

Come on, Norman, sit down.

OLIVER NILES

Hello. How are you?

NORMAN MAINE

Hi, Oliver.

A well-dressed lady comes up to Vicki at her table.

FEMALE SPEAKER

My dear, do let me congratulate you. You must be terribly proud and happy tonight.

VICKI LESTER

Thank you.

NORMAN MAINE

Somebody give me a drink.

Someone hands him a glass of wine, and he drinks it down.

Switch to the couple's bedroom. Norman has passed out in an easy chair. Vicki, looking up at him sadly but compassionately, pulls off one of his shoes, setting it down next to the Oscar statuette lying on its side.

Now we are in Vicki's dressing room. She is in costume, and Oliver comes in.

VICKI LESTER

Oliver, nice of you to come to my dressing room.

OLIVER NILES

Vicki, how are you?

VICKI LESTER

I missed you. Everyone's missed you. Have a nice trip?

OLIVER NILES

Well, a three months' tour of the theater circuit scarcely comes under the head of pleasure. But the way they're screaming for your pictures all over the country. Ms. Lester, if I may talk sharp, you are a knockout.

VICKI LESTER

Thank you. It's good to hear that.

OLIVER NILES

You've been crying.

VICKI LESTER

A little.

OLIVER NILES

How's Norman?

VICKI LESTER

Well, he's trying awfully hard, Oliver.

OLIVER NILES

Letting Norman leave this studio was the hardest thing I ever did. There was nothing else I could do.

VICKI LESTER

I know.

OLIVER NILES

Has he been . . . is he all right?

VICKI LESTER

He's gone to a sanitarium. He really wants to stop drinking. And I think he could, only . . .

OLIVER NILES

Well, perhaps if he could start working again, there would be some encouragement.

VICKI LESTER

Oliver, could you, could you do that?

OLIVER

Yes.

VICKI LESTER

Oh, thank you. But he mustn't ever know I told you.

OLIVER NILES

He won't know, and you mustn't worry. I want you to keep up your good work in this picture.

VICKI LESTER

I'll try, Oliver. That's the one thing I can do for you.

She hangs her head, and he takes her by the shoulders.

In the reception room of the sanitarium, Oliver enters, still wearing his hat, accompanied by Cuddles, an attendant.

CUDDLES

If you'll just sit here, Mr. Niles, I'll have Mr. Maine brought down.

OLIVER NILES
(taking off his hat)

Brought down?

Oliver looks around him and takes off his hat. Cuddles leads Norman downstairs into the reception room.

NORMAN MAINE

Hello Oliver, welcome to Liberty Hall.

OLIVER NILES

Hello, Norman.

NORMAN MAINE

Mr. Niles isn't slipping me a case of Scotch, Cuddles. This is just a handshake. This is Cuddles, Oliver, my social secretary. We go everywhere together.

OLIVER NILES

How are you feeling, Norman?

NORMAN MAINE

Fine, getting along remarkably well, Cuddles tells me. He says, you ought to see some of the boys. Let's sit down. Cuddles, we really don't need you.

Ignoring him, Cuddles sits down with them and leans forward with an intent but rather idiotic smile on his face.

NORMAN MAINE

Touching, isn't it? Can't bear to have me out of his sight.

OLIVER NILES

Are you comfortable here, Norman?

NORMAN MAINE

Comfortable? It's positively luxurious. They even have iron bars in the windows to keep out the draft.

OLIVER NILES

How much longer are you going to be here?

NORMAN MAINE

Oh, well, I'm really cured now. I'm just staying on for an extra week or two to get in good shape. You know, after all I'm in no particular hurry to return to the cameras.

OLIVER NILES

That's what I wanted to talk to you about. I've got a script with a fine part for you in it.

NORMAN MAINE

Oliver, that's great. That's great. Oh, who plays opposite me?

OLIVER NILES

Well, it is not exactly the lead, young Pemberton's doing that. But I tell you frankly, I consider your part better than the lead.

NORMAN MAINE

Oh, I see. It's better than, than the lead.

OLIVER NILES

Of course, it isn't terribly long, but it's one of those parts that makes an impression on you. They'll be thinking about you all through the picture.

NORMAN MAINE

Mm-hmm. Well, the thing is, Oliver, I'm pretty well set at another studio. And I'm not at liberty at the moment to tell you which one. You know yourself how those things are.

OLIVER NILES

Of course.

NORMAN MAINE

But it's a big picture. It's one of the biggest of the year. And the part? Every actor in Hollywood would give his teeth to play.

OLIVER NILES

Well, that's fine, Norman. And naturally, that will tie you up for a while. But we won't get to this picture for some time. And perhaps if you want to consider it for later on, we'll be . . .

NORMAN MAINE

Well, I'll tell you, Oliver, you'd better not count on me. See, I've got several pictures lined up after this, and then they're talking to me about England. You know, they're doing some very interesting things over there, you know?

OLIVER NILES

Mm-hmm.

CUDDLES

Hey.

NORMAN MAINE

What is it, Cuddles? Speak right out. We all love you.

CUDDLES

Your dinner.

NORMAN MAINE

Oh. We dine at 5:30 here. Makes the nights longer.

OLIVER NILES

Well, goodbye, Norman. I'm glad to see you getting along so well.

NORMAN MAINE

I'll be out in no time. I'll have to introduce myself all over to a lot of people who don't know me when I'm not drinking. Goodbye.

OLIVER NILES

Goodbye, Noman.

NORMAN MAINE

Thanks for dropping in.

Oliver leaves, and Cuddles closes the door behind him.

NORMAN MAINE

Well, Cuddles, alone at last, eh?

A billboard announcing "Christmas Week Racing, Santa Anita Park." Fanfare.

We now see horses and jockeys lining up in the track. The camera pans up to the audience and around the track. Another fanfare.

In a waiting room at the racetrack, Norman comes in and see three actors he knows, Bert, Sam, and Marion.

NORMAN MAINE
Hello, Bert, Sam, how are you, Marion?

SAM
Hello.

MARION
Hello.

BERT
Hello, Norman.

NORMAN MAINE
Glad to see you.

Norman goes off toward the bar.

SAM
How I hate to run into these has-beens. They give me the creeps.

MARION
Me too.

BERT
He was good while he had it, and he had it quite a while.

Norman is now at the bar.

NORMAN MAINE

Hello?

BARTENDER

Hello. Mr. Maine. I haven't seen you in a long time.

NORMAN MAINE

Oh, I've been resting. Ginger ale, please.

BARTENDER

Ginger ale and what?

NORMAN MAINE

Ginger ale and ginger ale.

BARTENDER

A new leaf?

NORMAN MAINE

A whole new book. Thank you.

Matt Libby comes up to the bar and sits down a seat away from
Norman.

MATT LIBBY

Scotch, straight.

NORMAN MAINE

Hello, Libby.

MATT LIBBY

Why, it's Mr. America of yesteryear. Do they let you
wander about now without a keeper?

• 103 •

NORMAN MAINE

Oh, sure. I'm a trustee now. Didn't expect to find you at Santa Anita. What do they do with the actors while you're away?

MATT LIBBY

Oh, they cut them into slices and fry them with eggs. I suppose you'll be here all the time now that you've retired from the hurly-burly of the silver screen.

NORMAN MAINE

Well, living down in Malibu now, pretty lonesome with Esther away working all day.

MATT LIBBY

Well, I wouldn't squawk about that if I were you. It's nice to have somebody in the family making a living.

NORMAN MAINE

Oh, wait a minute, Libby, I don't want to forget that we're friends.

MATT LIBBY

Friends, my eye. Say, listen, I got you out of jams because I had to. It was my job, not because I was your friend. I don't like you and I never have liked you. Nothing made me happier than to see all those cute little pranks of yours finally catch up with you and land you on your celebrated face.

NORMAN MAINE

Pretty work, Libby. Always wait until they're down, then kick them.

MATT LIBBY

I don't feel sorry for you. You'll fix yourself nice and comfortable. You can live off your wife now. She'll buy you drinks and put up with you, even though nobody else will.

Norman punches Libby. Libby punches back and knocks Norman to the floor.

A crowd surrounds them, and two policemen come up. They help Norman to his feet.

POLICEMAN

Come on, drunk.

NORMAN MAINE

Hey, wait a minute, wait a minute.

POLICEMAN

Come on, outside for you, wise guy.

NORMAN MAINE

I'm Norman Maine.

POLICEMAN

Oh, that's not my fault.

MATT LIBBY

Don't bother to toss him out. He's harmless.

POLICEMAN

All right, Mr. Libby, if you say so.

MATT LIBBY

Sure, let him go. What can he do? He can't fight any better than he can act.

FEMALE SPEAKER

It's Norman Maine!

Hubbub. The crowd disperses, and more people come in from the track. Norman goes back to the bar.

NORMAN MAINE

Give me a Scotch, double. Leave the bottle here.

We are now in Norman's house. There is a Christmas tree in the background. Vicki is standing with Oliver.

OLIVER NILES

Vicki, you'll be ill. Why don't you try to get a little sleep?

VICKI LESTER

But he's been gone four days. Four days, and not a word.

The phone rings.

VICKI LESTER

Oliver, I can't, I just can't.

Oliver answers.

OLIVER NILES

Hello? No, this is Oliver Niles speaking. What? Where? Thank you.

VICKI LESTER

What is it?

OLIVER NILES

Nothing. Nothing.

VICKI LESTER

Oliver, tell me.

OLIVER NILES

He's in the night court. He's been arrested on a drunk charge. Now he's all right. He isn't hurt. I'm going right down and get him out.

VICKI LESTER

I'm going with you.

OLIVER NILES

Vicki, it isn't any place for you. And if it gets in the papers . . .

VICKI LESTER

What do I care about the papers? I'm going with you.

Night court. Vicki is sitting in the audience. Norman is led in among a group of other suspects.

COURT CLERK

Division 30. Municipal Court County, Los Angeles, now in session. The honorable Judge George J. Parris presiding. Be seated, please.

Oliver approaches and sits down next to Vicki.

VICKI LESTER

Were you able to do anything?

OLIVER NILES

The judge wouldn't even see me.

COURT CLERK

Ready, your honor.

The judge addresses the suspects.

JUDGE GEORGE J. PARRIS

I want to advise you that you're entitled to be represented by counsel, to be confronted by the witnesses that may testify against you, to compel witnesses to attend on your behalf, to a public and speedy trial by the court, by a jury, and the right to be admitted to bail. Call the first five.

COURT CLERK

Gregory, Rails, Maine, Rodriguez, Johnson. Come on boys, go ahead. Move on.

Oliver sits down next to Vicki. They observe anxiously. Gregory, an aged drunk, is led to the bar. He is still drunk.

COURT CLERK

William Gregory, plain drunk. Picked up at Fifth and Towne, asleep in the gutter. 14 similar offences in the past six months.

JUDGE GEORGE J. PARRIS

Still at it, Gregory. How do you plead?

WILLIAM GREGORY

I don't feel too good.

JUDGE GEORGE J. PARRIS

I didn't ask you how you feel. I ask you how you plead?

WILLIAM GREGORY

Guilty, I guess.

JUDGE GEORGE J. PARRIS

When did you get out the last time?

WILLIAM GREGORY

Seven days before Christmas.

JUDGE GEORGE J. PARRIS

Well, I'm sorry you'll have to miss New Year's, but you'll be out in time for Washington's birthday. 60 days. Milton Rails.

Gregory is led off. Another suspect, Rails, is led to the bar. He is a young man, beaten up and with a bandage around his head.

COURT CLERK

A plain drunk, picked up on Brooklyn Avenue, given treatment at receiving hospital, then removed to jail.

JUDGE GEORGE J. PARRIS

How old are you, Rails?

MILTON RAILS

17, sir.

JUDGE GEORGE J. PARRIS

Did you take a good look at those men in the cell with you last night?

MILTON RAILS

Yes, sir.

JUDGE GEORGE J. PARRIS

And have you taken a good look at yourself this morning?

MILTON RAILS

No sir.

JUDGE GEORGE J. PARRIS

I suggest that you do. $5 and two days. Sentence
suspended.

MILTON RAILS

Oh, judge . . .

Rails is led off.

JUDGE GEORGE J. PARRIS

Alfred Hinkel, more commonly known as Norman
Maine.

Norman is led to the bar.

COURT CLERK

Drunk and disorderly, cracked car into tree at Sun-
set and Coronado; evidently been drinking for days,
resisted arrest and injured one of the arresting officers.

JUDGE GEORGE J. PARRIS

How do you plead?

ALFRED HINKEL

Guilty.

JUDGE GEORGE J. PARRIS

You're Norman Maine the actor, aren't you? You've
come pretty low, haven't you? There isn't a man here
who's had the advantages you've had. Look what you've
done with them. You're nothing but an irresponsible
drunk, driving about the streets with the power to
inflict death or injury on innocent people. I think we'd
better deny you that power for a while. 90 days in the
city jail.

ESTHER HINKEL

Please wait. I'm his wife.

Vicki moves up and stands next to Norman.

JUDGE GEORGE J. PARRIS

Yes, I recognize you, Miss Lester.

ESTHER HINKEL

Please, judge. I promise you this won't happen again. I'll be responsible for him if you just won't send him there.

JUDGE GEORGE J. PARRIS

Do you realize that this man, when drunk, is obviously a menace to public safety? And do you realize too, Miss Lester, the responsibility you'll be assuming to this court and to the commonwealth?

ESTHER HINKEL

I do.

JUDGE GEORGE J. PARRIS

Sentence suspended, prisoner remanded in the custody of wife.

ESTHER HINKEL

Thank you.

POLICEMAN

You can get him at the jail entrance, madam.

Norman is led off. Oliver comes up to Vicki and leads her away too. Rodriguez, a middle-aged Hispanic, is led to the bar.

COURT CLERK
(voiceover)

Jose Rodriguez. Plain drunk, picked up at First and
Main. Second offense.

JUDGE GEORGE J. PARRIS

How do you plead?

JOSE RODRIQUEZ

I think I'm guilty, your Honor.

JUDGE GEORGE J. PARRIS

60 days.

Now we see a wreath with the lights "Happy New Year." Behind
on the window, is "Police Dept. Division, 180-A." It is on a door,
which opens. A policeman exits and goes up stairs next to it.

Coming down the staircase next to this are Vicki and Oliver,
looking sad. Two policemen bring in Norman. Vicki goes up
to him.

NORMAN MAINE

I am so tired of this . . .

A group of photographers rush up to Vicki and Norman and
start taking pictures.

PHOTOGRAPHER

Hold it, Mr. Maine. Picture.

NORMAN MAINE

Oh, no.

JOURNALIST

What about a statement for the press?

NORMAN MAINE

No, please . . .

Now we see The Los Angeles Daily Press with the headline, "Norman Maine Released to Custody of Vicki Lester after Drunk Conviction! Night Court Drama as Star Pleads for Husband's Freedom."

Back in the living room of the Maine house, Vicki comes out of the bedroom.

VICKI LESTER

He's still asleep, been asleep nearly all day.

OLIVER NILES

That's the best thing for him.

VICKI LESTER

It's awful to see this happen to someone you love and know in your heart that it can't get any better. I only know that all I can do now is stay with him and try to help him.

The door to the bedroom is ajar. We see Norman, lying in bed, overhearing this conversation. He looks deeply disturbed. Back in the living room:

OLIVER NILES

So will I. And between us, we'll take care of him.

VICKI LESTER

You're very fond of him, aren't you, Oliver?

OLIVER NILES

I'm very fond of both of you.

VICKI LESTER

Then I know you'll understand what I have to tell you. And after what happened last night, I think you already know what it is. I can't do any more pictures. I'm going away for good with Norman.

OLIVER NILES

You can't do that, Vicki. You're at the very peak of your success, and you've worked so hard to achieve it.

VICKI LESTER

That's what's been wrong. I've thought it all out. Maybe if I hadn't been away from him so much, last night and what went before it wouldn't have happened. Well, I know it's too late to think about that now, but it may not be too late to go away with him and start over somewhere.

OLIVER NILES

It's your life you're giving up, Vicki.

VICKI LESTER

So I can try to give Norman back his. Can you honestly tell me I'm wrong to do it?

OLIVER NILES

No, Vicki, I cannot honestly tell you that.

VICKI LESTER

Then there'll be no more Vicki Lester.

OLIVER NILES

Come on, walk to the door with me. Goodbye, Vicki Lester. You were a grand girl. Good luck, Mrs. Norman Maine.

MRS. NORMAN MAINE

Goodbye.

Oliver goes out. Vicki walks around the living room in emotional pain and sits down despondently. She looks at the Oscar in the cabinet and breaks down crying. Norman comes out of the bedroom in his bathrobe.

NORMAN MAINE

Hey, darling, this is Maine, coming in to apologize again.

ESTHER HINKEL

I'm sorry, dear, but it isn't you.

NORMAN MAINE

What other troubles have you got?

ESTHER HINKEL

None. I was just playing a scene with myself.

NORMAN MAINE

Now look, I'm just coming out of the jitters and you are just going into them. This is a swell household.

ESTHER HINKEL

Isn't it?

NORMAN MAINE

I tell you what we'll do. I'll promise to brace up if you'll go on the wagon.

ESTHER HINKEL

I guess I have been drinking too much.

NORMAN MAINE

You know what I'm going to do? I'm going to be an athlete.

ESTHER HINKEL

You mean with great big muscles and everything?

NORMAN MAINE

Well, roughly speaking.

ESTHER HINKEL

Going to join the YMCA?

NORMAN MAINE

No, it costs too much. I'm going wading out in our front yard. Sure.

ESTHER HINKEL

Would you like me to go with you?

NORMAN MAINE

Sure. If you'd like to.

ESTHER HINKEL

Normy, I don't think I will. It might spoil this beautiful natural wave.

NORMAN MAINE

Yeah, I guess that's right. Darling. Look, could you have a hot toddy—I mean some hot soup—for me when I come back?

ESTHER HINKEL

Some hot soup.

NORMAN MAINE

Yeah. And I'll make some of those nice sandwiches.

ESTHER HINKEL

Normy, do you have to?

They laugh and hug, but Norman has a despondent expression.

NORMAN MAINE

Go on.

ESTHER HINKEL

Don't stay in too long.

Norman looks out at the sun setting over the waves of Malibu. Vicki is going into the kitchen when he stops her.

NORMAN MAINE

Hey! Do you mind if I take just one more look?

They exchange loving glances. She goes out, and he goes through the French door toward the ocean, closing it behind him.

Now a shot of Norman's feet on the beach. He takes off his sandals and robe, and we see him dive into the ocean. On shore, the waves begin to wash the robe and slippers away.

The screen now shows a headline from the Los Angeles Daily Dispatch: "Norman Maine's Body Found Off Malibu; Ex-Star Perishes in Tragic Accident! Wife, Vicki Lester, Overcome by Grief!"

Carnival music is anomalously playing.

Matt Libby is looking at it, seated at a bar.

MATT LIBBY

First drink of water he had in 20 years and then he had to get it by accident.

BARTENDER

[Laugh].

MATT LIBBY

Pardon me. How do you wire congratulations to the Pacific Ocean?

BARTENDER

[Laugh]

We now see Norman's funeral procession leaving a church. Dressed in mourning and with a veil over her face, Vicki is being led out by Oliver and Danny. There is a large crowd in front, some of them shouting at her as they proceed down the stairs.

WOMAN 1

There she is now!

WOMAN 2

You can't see her face.

FEMALE SPEAKER

Hello, Vicki.

The three descend into the crowd. Danny tries to protect her.

DANIEL "DANNY" MCGUIRE

Get away, can't you?

FEMALE SPEAKER 1

Come on Vicki, let's see your face!

Vicki, will you sign my book for me? Write, "Mrs. Norman Maine."

MALE SPEAKER

Don't you care, Vicki, you'll get over it.

DANIEL "DANNY" MCGUIRE

Stand back, can't you?

As they proceed toward the limousine, one woman in the crowd shouts:

WOMAN

Don't you cry, dearie, he wasn't so much.

Vicki screams and breaks down.

Back in the Maine house, Vicki, still in mourning, picks up a picture of Norman with a pipe and wearing a sweater. She walks around the room. All of the furniture is draped in sheets. She picks up the picture again.

VICKI LESTER

Do you mind if I take just one more look?

She puts the mourning veil over her face.

In the living room, the furniture is now covered with sheets. A female major domo is addressing Graves, a butler in white tie.

FEMALE MAJOR DOMO

Here are the paychecks for the servants, Graves. You'll find a very nice bonus in each one. Ms. Lester asked me to thank you for your kindness and service.

GRAVES

If there's anything I can do for the little lady, I should be glad to do it.

FEMALE SPEAKER

She would appreciate your attending to the closing of the Beverly Hills house.

Grandmother Lettie Blodgett comes in, followed by a couple of men carrying trunks.

GRANDMOTHER LETTIE BLODGETT

Put down those trunks. Put them down, I say. Well, where is she?

MAJOR DOMO

In the bedroom. Who are you?

GRANDMOTHER LETTIE BLODGETT

I'm her grandmother.

(to the porters)

Get out of the way.

Esther rushes into the room and embraces her.

ESTHER HINKEL

Granny, darling!

GRANDMOTHER LETTIE BLODGETT

Esther, darling.

ESTHER HINKEL

Oh, I'm so glad to see you. What made you come?

GRANDMOTHER LETTIE BLODGETT

Oh, I know when I'm needed.

(to the servants)

Now, get out of here. Go on, get out of here, all of you. I want to talk to my granddaughter alone. I came just as quickly as I could.

ESTHER HINKEL

But I'm going home. I sent you a wire yesterday.

GRANDMOTHER LETTIE

Hmph!

Grandmother Lettie pulls a sheet off the sofa and points to it. Esther sits down.

GRANDMOTHER LETTIE BLODGETT

Sit down. Is it true that you're going to quit the movies?

ESTHER HINKEL

I never want to hear of them again.

Grandmother Lettie sits down next to her.

GRANDMOTHER LETTIE BLODGETT

What are you running away from, dear?

ESTHER HINKEL

I'm not running away. It's just that I can't go on my heart isn't in it anymore.

GRANDMOTHER LETTIE BLODGETT

Once I told you, if you get what you want, you have to give your heart in exchange. And you said you were willing. Do you remember?

ESTHER HINKEL

I remember.

GRANDMOTHER LETTIE BLODGETT

It seems to me that you got more than you bargained for more fame, more success, even more personal happiness, maybe more unhappiness. But you did make a bargain and now you are whining over it. I don't think I'd feel so very proud of myself if I were you, Esther.

ESTHER HINKEL

I'm not, Granny, but my mind's made up.

GRANDMOTHER LETTIE BLODGETT

And I'm sorry I gave you the money to come out here. It was just a waste.

ESTHER HINKEL

Oh, but Granny . . .

GRANDMOTHER LETTIE BLODGETT

I was proud of you, Esther. I was proud to be the grandmother of Vicki Lester. It gave me something to live for. Now I haven't anything.

ESTHER HINKEL

I know. I want to be strong, but I can't go on. I can't.

GRANDMOTHER LETTIE BLODGETT

You must. Tragedy is a test of courage. If you can meet it bravely, it'll leave you bigger than it found you. If not, then you'll have to live all your life as a coward. Because no matter where you may run, you can never run away from yourself. I never knew Norman Maine. He wrote me a very sweet letter when you were married. He said, you told him how much I meant to you, and I know just how much you must have meant to him. You know, Esther, I can't believe that whatever he is, he can be very happy knowing that his death broke the spirit of the little girl he praised me so highly for raising, and I can't believe that he can be very proud knowing that all his great love did for you was to make you a quitter.

The major domo comes in.

MAJOR DOMO

The car is ready, Ms. Lester. We'll have to go now to make the train.

ESTHER HINKEL

Put the car back in the garage. Granny!

Grandmother Lettie and Vicki hug and cry.

A long shot of Grauman's Chinese Theater, with the name "Vicki Lester" up in lights.

ANNOUNCER

The entire picture industry has come to the Chinese theater for this opening tonight. It has come to pay tribute to a great star on a long-awaited return to the screen in what has been called her greatest performance. It has come to pay tribute to the girl herself, the girl who has won the heart of Hollywood. The girl who has won the heart of the world, Miss Vicki Lester. And if I'm not mistaken, Miss Lester's car has just driven up. Yes, it is she.

A limousine pulls up to the theater entrance, where there is a crowd. Danny, in black tie, gets out of the limousine and helps Grandmother Lettie out; she is wearing a mink stole. Vicki follows out of the car, to much applause. She looks pained but brightens at the applause.

DANIEL "DANNY" MCGUIRE
(to Grandmother Lettie)
I hope this doesn't scare you too much.

GRANDMOTHER LETTIE BLODGETT
I scare very slowly, young man.

Vicki is behind, escorted by Oliver.

PHOTOGRAPHER
Fix smile, folks, please.

DANIEL "DANNY" MCGUIRE
(to Grandmother Lettie)
They'll have your mug, I mean, your face plastered across half the papers in the country tomorrow.

GRANDMOTHER LETTIE BLODGETT
Hmm. How do I look?

DANIEL "DANNY" MCGUIRE
Oh, you look swell.

GRANDMOTHER LETTIE BLODGETT
You're a liar, but I like you.

ANNOUNCER
And here's Ms. Lester's, grandmother. Won't you say a few words to the radio audience, please?

DANIEL "DANNY" MCGUIRE
Say something, lady.

GRANDMOTHER LETTIE BLODGETT
You know, we've got a thing like that back home where they all listen in on, but we call it a party line. *[Laugh]*

Won't you say something, please; they're listening.

GRANDMOTHER LETTIE BLODGETT

Maybe some of you people listening in dream about coming to Hollywood, and maybe some of you get pretty discouraged. Well, when you do, you just think about me. It took me over 70—60—years to get here. But here I am. And here I mean to stay.

Laughs and applause for the audience. Oliver escorts Vicki forward. She stops short when she sees Norman's signature and footprints in the concrete. She balks, but Oliver bucks her up. The two walk proudly forward to a microphone.

ANNOUNCER

Miss Lester, this microphone is on an international hookup. Throughout the world, your fans are hoping that you'll say a few words to them.

VICKI LESTER

Hello everybody, this is Mrs. Norman Maine!

The ovation is tremendous. Tears are starting down her cheeks. She looks out past all this crowd, this confusion, this uproar, to some distant point of her own. The music swells up.

THE END

ABOUT THE FILM

Few Hollywood films have had the impact of the original version of *A Star Is Born*. Released in 1937 and starring Janet Gaynor and Fredric March, it was nominated for nine Academy Awards and won two (for best original story and best cinematography). Since then, the movie has been remade three times, attesting to its continued allure. But none have matched the genius and wit of the original.

A Star Is Born speaks to the longing for fame and its costs. Young Esther Blodgett leaves her home in North Dakota to make her way as an actress in Hollywood. She attracts the attention of cinema heartthrob Norman Maine, who not only falls in love with her but sees her star potential. He shepherds her through to acclaim.

In the meantime, Norman Maine's career plunges in the opposite direction. He was once a favorite leading man, but his alcoholism plunges him into escapades that embarrass the studio and destroy his talents as an actor. Esther's love for Norman is undying, but in the end she cannot protect him from himself.

This magnificent and poignant story illumines the ups and downs of celebrity—its pains, its pleasures, its glamor, and its uncertainties. We experience the splendor of Hollywood at the height of its Golden Age. We are also see the heartbreaks and tragedies that accompanied it.

This version offers a unique opportunity to enjoy this film complete in an audio format.

- The original dialogue from the film is reproduced complete.

- Accompanying narration enables the listener to vividly visualize the splendor of this Hollywood classic.

- This audio format enables listeners to create their own unique visual pictures of the movie.

- It is perfectly suited to those who love classic cinema but often don't have the time to sit down and watch a feature film.

- Listeners can enjoy this superb tale while commuting, jogging, exercising, cooking, walking pets, or during countless other activities.

The ever-changing pace of current life is shaping and reshaping the way we experience media. This audio version offers a classic film in a form that is uniquely suited to our times and tastes.

www.ingramcontent.com/pod-product-compliance
Lightning Source LLC
Chambersburg PA
CBHW071157300726

48975CB00004B/1184